HELP FROM THE BARON

She did not know when she lost consciousness. She did not know that she was lifted, carried towards the edge of the terrace, then down steps to a small landing-stage where water lapped softly, then lowered into the water and held under. There were two men. One pulled her coat off one arm and started on the other; as vultures would peck off carrion flesh.

Then, abruptly, a third appeared.

"Let her go," he ordered softly. "Cops."

The men holding Francesca under the water gave her a quick shove. One thrust out his foot, to push her farther away from the steps. Then he turned and hurried after the others. A policeman, on patrol, not expecting to find sensational crime, but quite sure that he would have to move away some imprudent lovers clutching in the darkness, reached the head of the steps.

The current had carried the girl out of sight.

**Also by the same author,
and available in Coronet Books:**

The Baron Goes Fast
Sport for the Baron
The Baron and the Arrogant Artist
The Baron Goes A-Buying

Help from the Baron

John Creasey
as Anthony Morton

CORONET BOOKS
Hodder and Stoughton

Copyright 1955 John Creasey

First published in Great Britain by
Hodder and Stoughton Limited 1955

Coronet edition 1961
Second impression 1970
Third impression 1975

The characters and situations in this book are
entirely imaginary and bear no relation to any real
person or actual happening

This book is sold subject to the condition that
it shall not, by way of trade or otherwise, be
lent, re-sold, hired out or otherwise circulated
without the publisher's prior consent in any
form of binding or cover other than that in
which this is published and without a similar
condition including this condition being
imposed on the subsequent purchaser.

Printed and bound in Great Britain for
Coronet Books, Hodder and Stoughton,
St. Paul's House, Warwick Lane,
London, EC4P 4AH
By Richard Clay (The Chaucer Press), Ltd.,
Bungay, Suffolk

ISBN 0 340 12949 2

CONTENTS

Chapter		Page
1.	The Body in the River	7
2.	Day into Night	12
3.	The Station and the River	21
4.	The Chances of Survival	27
5.	The Worried Young Man	35
6.	Consultation with an Expert	44
7.	A Man and his Friends	51
8.	A Half-tale of a Frightened Man	59
9.	The Representative of Big Interests	66
10.	The Whisper of Suspicion	73
11.	Mannering gets Home Late	80
12.	Mannering misses a Party	88
13.	A Visit to Ephraim Scoby	95
14.	A Detective gives a Warning	101
15.	The Curiosity of a Red-head	110
16.	A Welcome Home for Mannering	115
17.	An Ordeal for Francesca Lisle	123
18.	A Measure of Agreement	129
19.	Mannering Receives Instructions	136
20.	News from the Sûreté Générale	143
21.	A Visit by Night	151
22.	93 Forth Road	158
23.	The Final Fear of All	166
24.	The Return of Joy	172
25.	The Love of Francesca	180

1
THE BODY IN THE RIVER

BODIES seldom get into the River Thames by accident, although it is true that few days pass when at least one is not taken from the indifferent waters of London's river. Most of these are found between Putney—where on a day in spring the Oxford and Cambridge boat-race starts and sixteen young stalwarts and two near-pigmies provide delight, excitement, exercise of lungs and larynx for a million partisan Londoners—and Tilbury Docks. Of every dozen bodies found between these two points, at least six are pulled from the river by the River Police within a short distance of that crowded stretch of water between Westminster Bridge and Tower Bridge.

These facts preoccupy very few people. The Press takes a hopeful interest, but only the police trouble to make a record and turn a corpse into a series of notes on an index card. The police are never surprised to find a corpse. To the river patrols it is almost a matter of course to change direction, use the boat-hook, haul the body in and proceed to the nearest landing-stage. The first thing they do, of course, is to make sure that they have in fact found a *corpus*, that life is truly extinct, and that artificial respiration will do nothing to resuscitate the unhappy victim of circumstances.

So rigid are the ways of the London police, whether of the River, the City or the Metropolitan area, that the deceased is not officially considered to have passed on until a police-surgeon or, in extremity, some other doctor, has formally pronounced that life is extinct. From that moment onwards the discovery is a matter for investigation; often some surprising facts are discovered about the circumstances which led to the extinguishing of life.

Few men knew more about the variety of contributory

causes than Sergeant Worraby, of the River Police, Westminster Division.

Youthful officers on patrol with him on one of the fast police launches frequently declare that Worraby must be able to smell death at a distance. They say this admiringly. He will nose the bows of the launch towards a certain spot, call for the searchlight to be switched on, and stand heavy-footed in the thwarts while the inexperienced ply the boat-hook under his directions. His varied, extensive and colourful vocabulary is never really abusive; simply expressive.

The truth is that Worraby knows the River as another man might know a country lane or the vegetable garden at the back of his house in Muswell Hill or Wembley. He knows each little eddy; each drift of the current; every spot where a body will fetch up at high tide; every spot where it is likely to be rolling at low-tide. Being a conscientious officer, he invariably inspects these prospective watery graves, and so helps his legendary reputation to become a little more fabulous.

Worraby seldom talks about his prescience, his knowledge or his discoveries, although after the third pint—or, at Christmas and festive occasions, his second port—he will sometimes start to confide. Once launched, he is difficult to stop, and it is perhaps as well that he is an abstemious man by training. To look at, he is just another police-sergeant, a little on the plump side, fifty-seven years old and three years off retirement; grey-haired, clean-shaven, heavy beneath the jaws, with tired, patient grey eyes.

Many things are said about Worraby, the most persistent being that he needs only to glance at a corpse beneath the demoralising light of the launch's searchlight to be able to say—as he invariably does:

"Obvious case of *felo de se*, my lad", or "Homicidal victim, no one ever did that to himself", or "Lay you ten to one that he wasn't dead when he hit the water." Like a doctor diagnosing childish complaints, one glance is all that Worraby needs. He is seldom proved wrong At public expense, doctors who are already far too busy with the living are nevertheless employed to dissect certain parts of the anatomy of the corpse, write out extensive reports, then give evidence at long and often wearisome inquests; and the verdicts almost invariably concur with Sergeant Worraby's original: "I can tell you what happened to him, my lad—hit over the head and thrown in. Give you ten to one they tossed him in from Gimble's Steps." Or Fisherman's Bottom, Tickerton's Wharf, Moss Lane or any of a dozen romantically-named places. He has found by a mixture of experience and experiment that when a body or heavy object fetches up at a certain place, it enters the river at a point which could be specified.

Up and down the Thames, at the Thameside Divisions and at Scotland Yard, there is a kind of catch-phrase: "Ask Worraby, he'll know." And they ask, and he knows.

He was aware of and proud of his reputation, although, being a Cockney born and bred, and the sixth son of a family of eleven in the days when men were men and women had few opportunities to wear the trousers, he was not conceited.

Although he would never admit it, and probably would not even think of it, the truth is that he loves the Thames. He loves the smells—fish near Billingsgate, oil at Tilbury, spices at the Pool, where the ships come in from distant lands—from the Isle of Spices itself, or Mozambique, from the Gulf of Aden, from the hot-blooded lands of the Middle East and the dreamed-of countries like India and Pakistan, from little-known islands and from great continents. Fish, petrol and spices, then; or tea being unloaded into bond, coffee from Brazil or Africa, wool from the Antipodes and cotton from Egypt, from Africa or from the United States, tobacco from Rhodesia and Virginia, or a dozen places. It was said that Worraby had only to sniff the river breeze as a laden cargo-boat passed to say where she came from and what she carried, what her tonnage was, whether her crew were lascars, Chinese, Malays, white men, Dutch or Greek, French or Madagascan.

There were the warehouses, some topped by flaming

neon signs at night, others dark and gloomy. The broken skyline of the south bank, the more aristocratic outline of the north; the long bridges; the spots where small boys dived into the water on warm nights; the tiny beaches; the wharfs, docks, barges, pleasure boats, buoys, dinghies, the flotsam and jetsam, the places where the mist first gathered before fog spread in earnest over the river's broad, soft bosom—all of these were part of Sergeant Worraby's life, his past, his present and his future. It is unlikely that he ever thought of the word "romance" except in terms of boy and girl and the pictures, which he visited once a week with his capable wife, but he was part of the weft and weave of London's romance; he was truly alive at the pulsating heart of the world.

On the night of March 11th, a misty one when the fog was unlikely to become thick enough to worry about seriously, Sergeant Worraby sat in the bows of the Police Launch, A45, called an order, and saw the muddy bank looming up slowly through the mist near Bad Man's Steps. He called for the searchlight and, as it sprang out and struck the mist so that it looked as if a giant were breathing his hot breath over the river, he saw the body of the girl.

Worraby jumped up.

"Easy there! Jem, gimme that boat-hook, she hasn't been in long. Swing her round, Charley."

She was probably a pretty girl. She lay on her back, rolling very gently, as if floating in her sleep, bumping softly against the granite sides of Bad Man's Steps. Her long, fair hair spread out on the water, mist enshrouded her, her eyes were closed and her mouth slightly open. Scummy water lapped against her face, ran into her mouth and trickled out again.

"Hold it," ordered Sergeant Worraby, boat-hook in hands and one foot on the gunwale. In spite of his sixteen stones, he could balance as neatly as any tight-rope walker. The boat-hook caught in the dress at the girl's waist at the first attempt. Worraby drew her slowly towards the side of the boat, careful not to let her roll over.

Jem, otherwise Police-constable Norton, breathed on Worraby's neck.

"Proper Sleeping Beauty you've hooked this time, Sarge."

"Never you mind whether she's a sleeping beauty or an ugly sister, you get on the radio-telephone and report." Worraby spoke as he knelt down, held the girl and began to haul her into the launch. No beginner could have done it so swiftly; he had hauled hundreds of lightweights in exactly like this, and he was always gentle. "And listen, say there's a chance she can be saved. I'm applying artificial respiration, better have a doctor at the landing-stage, get stimulants ready, all the usual drill. Report she's about twenty, wearing a cocktail dress worth plenty, fair-haired, height about five-five, probably entered the river near Festival Hall Steps, and," went on Sergeant Worraby, putting the girl gently in the narrow thwarts, "get to hell away from here and get a move on!"

As he knelt beside the girl, something rolled from the neck of her dress—looking like a little trail of silvery light. It caught the constable's eye, as well as Worraby's.

"What's that?"

Worraby roared: "Do you *want* me to report you as being so ruddy inquisitive that you neglect——?"

"Okay, okay," said Norton, "but what is it? Looks like a diamond to me."

It looked like a diamond to Worraby, too. He didn't pick it up, but began to work on the girl, glancing at the thing which had rolled away from her. It shimmered and scintillated, possessing a kind of fascination. It was as if life had gone out of the girl only to be trapped by the stone. It seemed too bright to be a phoney, Worraby mused, the size of a peanut, and worth a fortune if it were real.

He went on with the artificial respiration.

The launch was soon cutting through the water towards the landing-stage, half a mile up-river at Westminster Bridge.

Worraby didn't think much about the girl or her chances of survival, but didn't spare himself as he worked.

. . . . . .

It should have been a happy day for Francesca Lisle. It was her twenty-first birthday.

It had begun so well. The only shadow had been one which she had known about for a long time. Her father had some secret worry. She was fond of him, and even devoted, for in a strange way, he won devotion. She did not know what secret fear he lived with, although she knew that one existed. He was too honest to lie. Whole weeks, sometimes whole months would pass when the shadow was so pale that she almost forgot it; now and again it grew dark, heavy and threatening—even frightening, although she did not know why it should frighten her.

The day had begun like this. . . .

2

DAY INTO NIGHT

FRANCESCA's bedroom overlooked the Thames Embankment and the river, and she loved it. Sitting up in bed, she could see the trees and the fields of Battersea Park, the massive yellow colossus of the Power Station, belching white smoke like some monstrous man-made giant, the shimmering river, river craft moving at stately speed, here and there white gulls riding the water, brought here in the trail of some ship.

The bedroom was large, and touched with the charm she gave to everything. Furniture, furnishings, pictures and *decor* were all of her choosing. They had lived in this top-floor flat for a year, everything was still fresh, and the excitement of being here, of having so much that she wanted, was still very real to Francesca. Until they had moved here, there had been a shabby furnished apartment in Bloomsbury, very little money—but a curious kind of contentment. Until then, she had known that it was a struggle for her father to help her at the Slade, but a sacrifice he wanted to make; she had always been quite sure of that. He believed that her talent could grow into genius, and she had hoped he was right.

She still hoped!

She could remember the day when he had told her that some old, almost forgotten and supposedly worthless shares had rocketed in value, transforming them from comparative poverty to comparative wealth. Not for months afterwards had she realised that the wealth had brought the shadow. Only recently had she begun to wonder why.

"The responsibilities of wealth, Franky!" her father would say, and laugh at her. He could laugh with his eyes. "Forget it, and think about your *art*." He could scoff at that, too, without discouraging her.

There was a small attic room above the flat, used by earlier tenants as a studio, with a small north light. That was why they had chosen this particular place. On the night before her birthday, Francesca had worked into the small hours in artificial light she knew wasn't good. Her father hadn't disturbed her; when she had gone downstairs she had found a note saying he had gone to bed, and:

"Don't forget the party tomorrow."

It was the first party they had thrown here; nearly all the guests were friends of hers, mostly from the Slade. There were one or two neighbours, too, particularly the Mannerings, from Green Street, which wasn't far away. Lorna Mannering, whose exhibitions attracted exclusive crowds and won whole pages in the shiny journals like the *Sphere*, the *Tatler* and the *Sketch*, had admired Francesca's *Head of a Bus Driver*, been friendly, invited her to her studio and introduced her husband. John Mannering's reputation in other spheres was as great as his wife's in the world of painting. Francesca had been to the Mannerings for tea two or three times, at cocktail parties twice.

She hadn't told her father that she had invited them. He had left all arrangements to her and, for the past two days, been out most of the time. She had really invited the

Mannerings and another couple of young middle age because most of the Slade students would be too young for her father.

She woke that day with a start, to find the room bright with sunlight, and her father standing by the side of the bed, tea-tray in hand.

"My goodness, is it *late*?" She struggled up.

"Not too late," he said putting the tray down. He stood and looked at her, his eyes filled with a curious kind of hurt radiance. She often felt that he did feel hurt when looking at her, as if she reminded him of something precious but gone. She did, of course; her mother. Looking down at her like that, he was the most handsome man she knew, his hair touched with grey, his features so regular and distinctive; he didn't look English, more Continental. "Many, *many* happy returns of the day, my darling."

"Why, it's—*today*!"

"*She has the key of the door*," her father had started to sing, half-mockingly, "*never been twenty-one before*. Yes, the great day, Franky."

He poured out tea.

At her place, when she went into the dining-room for breakfast, was a small packet, tied up with pink ribbon.

"Never mind that until you've had breakfast!"

"But I couldn't eat!" She slipped the ribbon off, tore off the paper, found the small leather box and knew that this was a jewel, opened it—and saw a small jewelled cross lying against dark-blue velvet. The cross was so beautiful, so breathtaking, that she hadn't known what to say. She had just looked at her father, feeling the tears stinging her eyes.

Eventually: "But it's the loveliest thing I've ever seen! Diamonds, emeralds, rubies, sapphires——" She turned the gift this way and that, as if seeking to see every facet of its beauty. "But you shouldn't have——"

"It was your mother's," he said.

Then he swept her into talk about the party, the day itself, newspaper headlines, the Slade, the wisdom of going to Paris for a year for more study. If she went to Paris she would have to live in a garret. If she could stand a garret she would probably become a genius; if she couldn't——

"Why, how funny," she interrupted. "Mr. Mannering was saying that the other day, almost the same words." She glanced down at the jewelled cross, and didn't notice the change in her father's expression. "In Paris, genius and garrets go together, the life of a sybarite there or anywhere else can only waste——" Glancing up, she saw his expression. "Daddy, what is it?"

"Nothing, my dear."

"Don't be absurd, there is." Staring, she realised that he had looked like this once or twice before when she had mentioned the Mannerings; and she remembered, too, that when he'd been asked to go round and have a drink with them, he had found an excuse. "Daddy, why don't you like the Mannerings?"

"I don't even know them."

"That's what I mean!"

"Forget it, Franky."

"I wish you'd tell me," she said, "and I wish I'd realised before that you don't like them." She was genuinely upset. "If I'd only thought, I'd never have invited them."

Although he tried hard to hide it, hardness sprang into his eyes.

"Invite them here?"

"Yes, tonight. They've been so good, I wanted you to meet them." The jewelled cross, the mockery in his eyes, the happiness of the morning, were all gone; she was acutely distressed. "Daddy, I can't put them off now, can I?"

"My sweet, it's the last thing I'd want you to do."

"Why don't you want to meet them? Twice before you've avoided them, and I hadn't realised that."

He hesitated; then his face cleared and he leaned forward to the hot-plate, placed another rasher of bacon on her plate, brought that silent laughter to his eyes, and said:

"I'll tell you after I've met him."

"Promise?"

"Francesca," he said very suddenly, "I wish to God you hadn't to grow up."

.   .   .   .   .

There wasn't much time to think.

Her father had gone out in the middle of the morning, promising to come back in good time for tea. The one maid, worked up about the party, became temperamental. The tit-bits, ordered from a West End firm, were late in coming. Hired glasses, hired dishes, even the drinks hadn't arrived in the middle of the afternoon. One of the three hired waiters came with a dripping cold, and used a venomous tongue when she told him she just couldn't let him stay. It was after five before she realised that her father wasn't back.

He'd soon arrive.

He didn't arrive at all.

Minute by minute as the late afternoon had passed, she had waited and watched, but he hadn't come. The party was to last from six until eight o'clock. Three of her closest friends, two girls of her own age and a boy slightly younger, had arrived first, realised she was worried, and taken a lot of the burden off her shoulders. The party had soon warmed up, and become more hilarious than she had expected.

A second worry was added to her father's non-appearance; that when the Mannerings and others of the generation senior to this arrived, they would feel that it was like a bear-garden. Everyone was comparatively sedate so far, but two were talking far too much, and a red-haired girl with an enormous bust was talking much too loudly.

Then the Mannerings had arrived—John Mannering, tall, distinctive in a way which reminded her of her father, but as English as anyone could be. His good looks seemed to belong to an earlier age, needed a wide-brimmed cavalier's hat or the clothes of a Regency buck to set them off. And Lorna, his wife, was remarkable; the kind of woman one might hope to be. It wasn't only her looks, although she was quite handsome. Her expression? She could look haughty and be aloof. It was poise, perhaps, a manner which somehow made it obvious that she was nice to know. She had the figure of a young woman, moved lithely, and had as much dress sense as Dior.

It was easy to envy her.

Mannering was dashingly handsome, almost too spectacular; and this party wasn't right for him; or for Mrs. Mannering, either.

"It was crazy," thought Francesca. "I should never have asked them."

They shook hands, were natural and amiable, and moved freely among the mob. They hadn't been in the room five minutes before the ginger-haired girl burst into a screaming laugh.

". . . and my dear, you couldn't tell whether she was painting a corpse from the inside or the out!"

Francesca hated her.

The Mannerings didn't seem to notice. Francesca knew Lorna much better than John, but it was John who seemed to take the lead. His easy manner and ridiculous good looks fascinated both men and girls. He seemed to have comprehended the situation when she'd apologised for her father's absence, and glanced round occasionally at Francesca.

Suddenly and bewilderingly John Mannering became the lion of the evening. To students of the Slade, Lorna Mannering should have been, and gradually she drew their interest; but it was Mannering who seemed to sense the need, turned strident laughter into chuckling mirth, drew the timid out of nervous silence. The other couple in their late thirties arrived soon afterwards, and mixed smoothly; Francesca felt that she could breathe again.

She could think, too, and her only coherent thoughts, apart from the progress of the party, were about her father.

Could he be deliberately avoiding Mannering?

She kept looking at Mannering. He was taller than most of the men present, his dark hair was flecked with grey, which perhaps lent him the touch of distinction. His eyes, hazel in colour, could laugh much the same way as her father's.

A younger man, whom she had invited partly because of his sister, who was also at the Slade, was by her side when she caught Mannering's eye. Mannering looked away after a moment, but Francesca couldn't. She wasn't simply fascinated by Mannering; there was gnawing anxiety within her, and the unanswered question—whether her father had stayed away to avoid Mannering.

The younger man, Simon Lessing, thrust a glass into her hand.

"You haven't had a sip for twenty minutes, you'll be parched by the time it's all over. Like some nuts?"

"No, thank you, I——"

"Potato crisps? Caviare—what blatant luxury!—cheese straw—or try one of these shrimp patties, they're exactly the thing."

"No, I——"

"Come on, Franky, be human!"

Simon was grinning at her in a nice way. He was very like Joy, his sister, who was gay and full of vitality, and seemed to know everyone.

"Joy" was the right name for her. Both brother and sister had clear greeny-grey eyes, a short nose, generous lips. The lips were too full for a man, but—nice. And Lessing's short nose was peppered with freckles, his crisp brown hair waved a little.

She looked at him, and felt herself relaxing. Her father and Mannering could affect her the same way.

"Well, all right, a few chips."

"Or chipolatas on sticks?" He held out another dish, and she saw that he had refilled her glass; it was brimful. There was a ceaseless overtone of talk, the red-haired girl's occasional shrill laugh, a group round Mannering, and another round Lorna, a haze of smoke, everything that there should be. "You could slip out of the room and cool off, no one would know you'd gone. Sure sign of a successful party when one forgets one ought to be thinking of one's hostess."

"Nonsense."

"Fact. Cheers. I wonder if anyone besides Mannering has told you how lovely you look."

She flushed; it was unexpectedly good to flush.

"Idiot," she said, "and he didn't."

"Don't you believe it, those eyes were telling you all the time. Great chap, John Mannering. Did you know about his *alter ego*?"

"Eh?" She did; she didn't want to talk about it. "Simon, look, there are two girls over in that corner looking a bit forlorn, will you be an angel and go and rescue them?"

"No. Gifted family, the Mannerings, what with Lorna, who never puts paint to canvas for less than a hundred guineas, unless it's out of love for her subject, and Mannering, who runs the most exclusive antique shop in London—he actually has a couple of el Grecos there now—and who is the most knowledgeable private eye who ever winked at Scotland Yard. Fact. I could tell you some stories about Mannering——"

"Simon, *please* go and talk to those girls."

"Conditionally," Simon said. "That I may be the last to leave."

. . . . .

He had been the last to leave. After the Mannerings, after all the youngsters, even after red-haired Susan Pengelly of the balloon front, who was hardly able to stand upright when the evening was over, and wanted to stay all night. In fact, Simon sent Joy on with a boy-friend, and did not leave until nearly ten o'clock. They got on to painting, of course, he was a dabbler too. They went to the studio, and became so absorbed that several times and for minutes on end Francesca forgot her father.

When Simon had gone, she couldn't forget for a minute. The maid and the hired staff had cleared the flat, but it still looked forlorn, untidy, empty. She felt empty, too. She couldn't believe that her father would have let her down like this deliberately, and was beginning to feel frightened. Really frightened.

When the telephone bell rang, she flew to it.

"Hallo!"

"Franky, listen," said her father, and she went weak with relief. "I hate myself for what happened, but it was unavoidable. And I can't explain now. I want you to do something for me. It is extremely important."

Relief fought with fresh fears which the tone of his voice brought on.

"Are you there, Franky?"

"Yes. Yes, I'm here, what——?"

"Listen very carefully, Franky, please. Go into my bedroom, and pull up the carpet in the corner by the wardrobe. You needn't pull it back far. You'll see a loose floorboard. Prise that up, and take out the wash-leather bag you'll find inside. Understand, Franky?"

She felt like choking.

"Yes. Yes, I understand. Then what shall I do?"

"Bring the bag to me," her father said. "I'm at Waterloo Station, I have to catch the late train to Southampton. I'll be by the main bookstall—you know it well. Come as soon as you can, Franky."

"I—yes, I will."

"I'll explain when you get here," her father said, "goodbye for now, my darling."

He rang off.

Francesca hesitated—and then began to act with frenzied haste. She was ready, with the wash-leather bag, when Cissie came in, guiltily:

"Oh, Miss, there was this letter, it came during the party." She had a typewritten envelope in her hand, marked "Special delivery". "I expect it's someone who couldn't come——"

"Yes," Francesca said, huskily. She thrust the letter in her pocket. "Cissie, I want you to wait until I get back, sleep here the night if necessary." She took agreement for granted, and hurried out.

3

THE STATION AND THE RIVER

FRANCESCA sat in a corner of a taxi; still frightened. The wash-leather bag was in her handbag, clutched tightly in her hand. She had found it where her father had said she would, and hadn't put it down while telephoning for the taxi, or when slipping into a three-quarter-length sealskin coat and hurrying downstairs.

She had waited in a frenzy of impatience for the taxi.

The telephone call, the mystery and the new fears, added to the ordeal of waiting for him and the shock of disappointment, had affected her nerves much more than she realised. She was actually clenching her teeth and trembling when the taxi drew up. Yet she had noticed the car which moved after her, seeing its twin lights in the driver's mirror and feeling a sudden flare of hope that it was her father. She had jumped round, staring—and then remembered that she was going to meet him at Waterloo Station.

The car was still behind her.

They were passing the Houses of Parliament on one side, and an entrance to the Abbey on the other. The lighted streets were nearly empty, statues of dead famous men watched, the face of Big Ben was lighted, like the round, yellow face of a spirit on the night of Halloween. One could fancy a witch astride her broom clearing the pinnacle of the tower, screeching among the clouds over quiet London.

The taxi rattled and sped over Westminster Bridge. Floodlit buildings on the north bank sent a pale glow into the sky. She saw lights on the water, of a moving craft; and did not dream that, soon, a man on that police launch would see her floating, and pull her alongside. She was quite sure now that the other car was following her, and she clutched the handbag very tightly.

What was in the wash-leather bag?

Somehow, she knew. Jewels. Mannering was a famous connoisseur of jewels, her father wouldn't meet him. Jewels. She could remember an evening, not so long ago, when she'd read about a wealthy jewel merchant being robbed, and heard her father's chuckle.

"Why, what's funny?" she had asked.

"It was bound to happen sooner or later. You'd be surprised if you knew how many ordinary-looking men, usually old men into the bargain, carry a fortune in their pockets. Most often it's in a little wash-leather bag and a bit of cotton-wool."

"How do you know?"

"General knowledge, Franky, is part of living."

They were half-way over the bridge. By leaning to one side, Francesca could see the lights of the following car. Several others were also behind her, but she recognised this one because of the shape of the parking lights. It was a big car, and was speeding. It drew nearer, and she was suddenly afraid, opened her lips but strangled a scream.

The car passed.

One man, visible only as a pale blur, looked at her through the open window as it went by.

She found her handbag open, her fingers playing with the wash-leather, feeling something hard inside it. In a moment that was almost of frenzy, she untied the string which gathered the neck together, and dug her fingers inside. First she touched cotton-wool, and pulled this out; next, she felt the hardness again.

There were small, hard things wrapped in cotton-wool; dozens of them.

She unwrapped one, as the taxi passed a street-lamp. Such fiery light leapt from the diamond in her fingers that it dazzled her. Then the light fell behind her and the taxi became dull again.

She dropped the diamond.

The taxi swung round, on the main road again, and in a moment they would be approaching the station; she hadn't much time. She bent down, panicking, and then realised that if she wasn't careful she would drop other diamonds. She pulled the two ends of the string, fastening the bag again, clutched it tightly in her right hand, and groped for the single stone.

It was under her foot, painful through the thin sole.

She picked it up. Several taxis were roaring up the slope, not far ahead there was a cluster of red lights, where cabs and cars were putting down their passengers. If she opened her bag again, she would have a job to close it, and she wanted to be ready to jump out of the cab.

She slipped the diamond into the neck of her dress, thrust it deeper so that it was caught inside her brassiere, and then the taxi stopped and jolted her forward.

She felt hot and flustered when she got out, but no one took any notice of her. No private cars stood near by. She hurried across the hall towards the platforms. Hundreds of people were waiting about, as many hundreds were walking towards the different platforms—1 to 12 were this side of the station. The bookstall was a little to her right, only the news section open, with several customers standing there.

Francesca did not see her father.

She looked round, in desperation; he was not in sight, but she realised that several men were looking at her.

Simon Lessing would probably have told her that it was because of her looks; and certainly her flushed cheeks and scared eyes added sparkle to her beauty. But she did not think of those things, only felt scared of attracting attention. She let her hands fall by her side, and held her bag tightly but tried to appear casual. She moved nearer the bookstall, standing near the busy, brightly lit news counter, and scanned the station.

Her father was *not* here. Yet he had said that he was talking from Waterloo.

Then, suddenly, frighteningly, he spoke from behind her; from the shuttered side of the bookstall.

"Franky, don't look round. I'm here."

She started, violently.

"Speak very softly," her father said. Now, as on the

telephone, he spoke as if he had not a second to spare, as if every second were vital. "Did you get the bag?"

She whispered chokily: "Yes."

"Don't give it me now," he said. "I'm being watched and followed. Go down the escalator to the Tube trains, then come back again, then go across to the Festival Hall. You know, where we met last week. I'll join you there. If I haven't arrived in—in twenty minutes, go home and wait until you hear from me again."

"Dad, what——?"

"I'll tell you everything the moment I can," her father said. "Go now, Franky, please."

She looked about her again, playing a fantastic game of let's pretend, pretending to look for him although knowing exactly where he was. Then she moved towards the far side of the station and the escalator leading to the Underground. Once, she glanced round. She didn't see her father, but she did see a man, a bearded man, by the bookstall. Blindly, she went on, forgetting that she did not want to attract attention. Two men out of three turned to look at her. She was so young, and fear gave her cheeks a sparkling colour and put glowing lights into her eyes. She carried herself superbly, wore just the three-quarter-length coat over her white cocktail dress, with a tulle scarf at her throat. Her fair hair, at its best for the party, crowned true loveliness.

She did exactly as her father had told her.

Several times she looked round; but did not see him, and she saw no one who appeared to be following her. Throngs of people were coming up from the Tube, to catch late trains to the outer suburbs; most were couples, some of the young were holding hands. A middle-aged man with a bucolic face deliberately stepped into her path, raised his bowler hat and said: "Good-evening." She slipped past him. She waited for a few minutes, until another train emptied, then mixed with the crowd coming off that, and went back on to the main-line station.

One swift look round told her nothing.

She hurried towards the steps leading down into the

THE STATION AND THE RIVER

main entrance and the main road. Soon, she was crossing towards the Festival Hall. It was almost in darkness, but street-lights were on, and people were streaming from Hungerford Bridge—the footbridge—some running as if they feared that they would miss their train.

Only a few walked in Francesca's direction.

None of these was behind her.

She reached the entrance to the hall. Lights were on in the offices, people were working there, cleaners were sweeping, two men in bowler-hats and carrying furled umbrellas were deep in earnest conversation. She knew the exact spot where her father would meet her; beyond the shimmering entrance, nearer the terrace overlooking the river.

There it was dark; but across the river, the squat tower of the Shell Mex House and the square mass of the Savoy were still floodlit, lightening the dark sky over the city. All the time people thronged down the steps from Hungerford Bridge; twice a train rumbled over the railway section.

It was at the height of the rumbling that a man appeared close to Francesca, as if from nowhere.

"Miss Lisle?"

She spun round, hands raised, heart pounding. "Oh!"

"I'm so sorry to frighten you." He was well-spoken and he looked smart, dressed in a dark overcoat; a smiling man of thirty or so, wearing a trilby hat pulled forward over his face. "I think you're expecting your father."

"Yes, I am, but——"

"He's over here," the man said, and put a hand on her right arm.

She clutched her handbag more tightly in her right hand. The pressure of the man's fingers scared her, and she snatched her arm away.

"Where——?"

"If you want to see him alive again," the man said, without a change of tone, "you'll be wise to come with me. He'll be all right if you do, and you'll be all right too."

At first she hardly realised what he was saying. Then

she sensed, she *knew* that he meant it. The threat shocked her into submission. She let him take her arm and draw her towards the terrace. She wanted to scream and pull herself free, but there was that awful fear of what would happen if she did. The fears she had felt all day, the fears which had grown so dark and frightening during the party, came to a head.

Dozens of people were in sight, some certainly saw her. But what did they really see? A pretty girl and a young man, arm-in-arm now, moving out of the lighted footpath towards the darkness of the terrace.

Suddenly Francesca was out of the range of the bridge lights; of all lights except those across the river.

All she knew was fear.

Then, swiftly, a gloved hand went over her mouth, pressed hard and thrust her backwards. She tried to bite the hand, but her teeth slid over shiny leather. She kicked out, without knowing whether she struck her assailant or not. She felt suffocated. Her ears were filled with roaring and her head felt light; there was a dreadful tightness at her breast, she just couldn't breathe.

She couldn't *breathe*.

It was like going under an anæsthetic, with the awful fear that she would never come round.

. . . . . .

She did not know when she lost consciousness. She did not know that she was lifted, carried towards the edge of the terrace, then down steps to a small landing-stage where water lapped softly, then lowered into the water and held under. There were two men. One pulled her coat off one arm and started on the other; as vultures would peck off carrion flesh.

Then, abruptly, a third appeared.

"Let her go," he ordered softly. "Cops."

The men holding Francesca under the water gave her a quick shove. One thrust out his foot, to push her farther away from the steps. Then he turned and hurried after the others. A policeman, on patrol, not expecting to find sensational crime, but quite sure that he would have to move away some imprudent lovers clutching in the darkness, reached the head of the steps.

The current had carried the girl out of sight.

4

THE CHANCES OF SURVIVAL

"What are her chances?" Jem Norton asked.

He spoke to Sergeant Worraby as to an oracle, although the girl in the white dress had been lifted on to the landing-stage, and was already on a couch inside, with a doctor fiddling with a hypodermic syringe. Bright lights on the landing-stage which was snug against the embankment wall, showed Worraby as looking tired, with dark patches beneath his eyes.

"Wouldn't like to say," said Worraby. "Out of our hands now, anyway, and why don't you stop asking questions?" An Inspector came out of his office. From the habit of fifteen years as a regular soldier, Worraby drew himself up—but checked his salute, from the habit of twenty-three years as a policeman. "Evening, sir."

"Still keeping it up," remarked the Inspector.

"Trying to, sir."

"Nice work. You think she came in by the Festival Hall terrace, apparently."

"Ten to one on it, sir."

"You're probably right. Nip across and have a look round, will you? A Squad car's gone to have a look on the terrace, you'll probably see them there and on the steps. No harm in having a word with them."

"Right, sir."

"How long do you think she'd been in?"

"Not more'n an hour, sir, maybe not that," said Sergeant Worraby; he was a great believer in formality when with a senior officer. "She had a bit of luck, rolled over on her back and fetched up against those old cement bags—you know, sir, the place where a barge foundered and ten tons of cement went hard as a rock. Kept her on her back, that and the current just there."

"Well, she needed some luck," the Inspector said. "Anything else?"

"This, sir." Worraby shot out his right hand, opened it, and startled the Inspector and even made Jem Norton blink. Light stabbed from the grimy palm, so bright that it even surprised Worraby himself. He grinned. "Rolled out of the young woman's person, sir."

"What?"

"Neck of her dress, sir."

"Oh." The Inspector took it. They stood beneath those bright lights which surrounded the stage; no light could have been better for the diamond. There it lay, the size of a peanut cut in a hundred or more tiny facets; and each facet scintillated, giving off a different light and a different hue. It silenced three hardened men for fully half a minute. Then: "Hum," said the Inspector. "That might have been buried in the mud, that's her second piece of luck. Or someone's." His hand closed over the diamond. "All right, nip across to the Terrace Steps, will you? or we'll have those blasted landlubbers pinching all your glory."

Worraby kept a straight face. "Aye aye, sir," he said, and turned smartly and stepped into the launch. It was soon chugging off across the dark breadth of the Thames.

The Inspector turned away, his smile gone, and went towards the room where the girl lay. He went in. The doctor was not giving her an injection. The girl's face was turned towards the door, and the Inspector's thoughts were wrenched off the diamond. Even like that, mouth slack and eyes closed and a dribble of dirty Thames water coming out of her mouth, she was striking.

"Only a kid," he said, to no one in particular. "What are her chances?"

The doctor grunted.

"Eh?"

"What—oh, never mind." The Inspector glanced at the diamond, then looked back at the girl. He shook his head. He went into his office and telephoned the landlubbers, reporting the diamond. This was already a job for Scotland Yard, and the Yard would grouse like hell if any information were kept back even by half an hour. Once they had it they would probably sit on it all night, but there was no one to grouse at them.

The job done, he went back into the other room.

A policeman was covering the girl in blankets. The doctor stood against the wall, cigarette glowing at his lips, grey hair standing on end, sweat dropping from his forehead and upper lip. He had loosened his collar and tie, and the collar was soaked with sweat.

The Inspector's voice quickened with excitement.

"How is she?"

"If she dies, it won't be from drowning," the doctor said. "Get her to hospital, they should pull her through."

. . . . .

In spite of the long years of practice, Worraby was neither truly cynical nor superficially blasé, but a somewhat earnest man with unexpected quirks of humour and a natural ability to divine whenever his leg was being pulled. Hence his "Aye, aye, sir" to the Inspector. As the launch went straight across the smooth Thames, the steady chug-chug of the engine and the even splash of the water against the bows and broadside-on the only nearby sounds, he was wondering about that girl. Some girls depended on paint and powder for their looks, some depended on their vitality, just now and again a real beauty turned up. Something to do with bone structure, and this girl had it. She was young, too. If those two things weren't enough to make him ponder, there was the diamond.

"Sarge," said Jem Norton.

"What's up?"

"How much do you reckon that diamond was worth? Show it to my old woman, and she'd faint."

"Show it to mine, and she'd clout me, which is nothing to what I'd do to her," said Worraby, and sniffed. "I dunno. Thousand quid, probably."

"Blimey! Wholesale?"

"How the hell do you think I know if it's wholesale or retail, you mutton-headed son of a—and look here, what's the matter with you tonight? Anyone would think I was paid to answer the damn-fool questions of a damn-fool copper who—*what's that?*"

They were near the Terrace Steps. Two or three men were moving about at the top of the steps, and a light had been rigged up and was shining down into the water near the spot where the girl had been found. So the water shimmered. Worraby saw a dark patch in the midst of brightness, and spoke and moved as if he were twenty years younger. Before Norton realised what he was doing, Worraby was prodding at the something with a boat-hook.

Excitement faded.

"Only a cloth or something," Worraby said. "Heavy, though." He drew the thing close to the launch. "See what it is, a fur coat. Sealskin, ain't it? Gimme a hand, you clot." They hauled the dripping coat on board, then spread it out. Worraby ran the light of a torch over it, found a pocket and, trying to avoid kneeling on the sodden fur, inserted two fingers into the pocket.

Inside was a small purse of Moroccan leather, inside the purse a notice from the Slade school addressed to Miss Francesca Lisle, of 99b Riverside Walk, Chelsea. There was also a letter, in its envelope and sealed, addressed to the same person.

"You know, I wouldn't be surprised if that isn't hers," said Worraby, thoughtfully.

"*Found anything down there?*" bellowed a Squad car man from the terrace. He stood at full height, outlined against the flaming red of an advertisement for Oxo, and no grizzly bear could have looked more formidable.

THE CHANCES OF SURVIVAL

"*What's that?*" shouted Worraby. "Jem, put that stuff from the coat safe somewhere, will you?"

Jem Norton took the purse and dropped the letter when a man from the terrace yelled again:

"*Found anything?*"

"'*Course we've found something, why don't you chaps keep your eyes open?*" Worraby called back.

The Squad man chuckled.

"*Blind O'Riley if it isn't Sarge Worraby! Okay, sarge, you can keep it. After the lot we've found, we don't even want any more.*"

"Here, Jem," said Worraby to the man at the tiller, "get her alongside, I want a looksee." He kicked against the boat-hook, bent down to put it in its fixing, and didn't notice the letter that it fastened down.

The men on the Terrace hadn't found very much. There was a piece of cotton-wool, which looked as if something round and hard had been inside it for a long time; there was a little indentation on the inside. A cigarette-end, still damp, a few footprints made when a man had stepped into a muddy pool some way along, and some marks which looked as if a woman had been dragged along, with small heels scraping the ground.

The night was brightened with vivid flashes as they took photographs. Two men from the Division arrived with some plaster of Paris, hoping for casts of the footprints. Worraby and the Squad men chatted, all about shop, and Worraby talked of the diamond.

"That cotton-wool could have been wrapped round some sparklers," a Squad man said. "Might be some more of them. This looks like your big chance, Sarge, you might get promotion after all!"

Worraby didn't smile even faintly.

"Who wants promotion?" he asked. "All you have to do is try to teach a lot of dimwits like you. Better shove off, I think. Goo'-night."

He took the sealskin coat and the purse straight back to the landing-stage, together with the story of the cotton-wool and the other finds. Before he handed this over, he asked about the girl; he was really anxious.

"Got a good chance," said the Inspector, who was looking at a nylon slip. All the girl's wet clothes, including the cocktail dress, were on the bench. "Initials on this are F. L., nothing else was marked. She——"

"Francesca Lisle!" Worraby exploded.

"Got second sight now?"

Worraby handed over the purse, with the notice from the Slade, then remembered the letter. Jem Norton hadn't given it to him. He didn't say anything of it, but went back to look.

They searched everywhere, but couldn't find the letter. Worraby shifted everything in the thwarts, by the engine, on the seats, and Norton did the same as a double-check.

"Must 'a fallen overboard," Norton muttered. "I could kick myself, Sarge."

"Forget it," Worraby said, uneasily.

He didn't forget it, but reported verbally to his chief, without naming Norton as the culprit. His chief made a note, and told him not to worry about it. Worraby didn't; duty done as well as it could be now, he went on with his job.

That was the last thing that the River Police did in the investigation proper, but the Inspector, Worraby's chief, spoke to the Yard again. This time he found himself talking to the Yard's expert on precious stones, an old hand in Superintendent William Bristow.

Bristow was really an expert; and all who knew him voted him a man worth knowing. He was conscious of his own shortcomings, a sensitivity which actually helped to make him a good officer.

. . . . .

Bristow looked what he was; thorough, conscientious, human. His one bad habit was chain-smoking; a glance at his brown fingers and browned moustache—which was now grey in its natural state—betrayed that. He smoked a lot because he worried about his jobs; lived, ate, slept and had his leisure with difficult cases.

Bristow sent men to 99b Riverside Walk, found the maid

—Cissie—in sole possession, the party chaos still chaos after a fashion, the odour of tobacco smoke and spirits heavy everywhere. No one had thought of throwing a window up and letting some fresh air in.

The maid behaved well, when told a little of what had happened. She had a fairly straightforward story which might not help, but did enable Bristow to get a picture of a Francesca Lisle keenly disappointed because her father hadn't arrived for the party which had mattered so much, and rushing off when she'd had a telephone message.

"I feel sure it was from her dad, sir," the maid said.

"You're probably right." At times Bristow could be the most affable man at the Yard. "How many guests were there, do you say?"

"Oh, exactly fifty-three, sir. Miss Francesca wanted to have as many as she could, that's why it was a cocktail party. We couldn't seat more than a dozen at the table, and she has such a lot of friends, she's ever so nice." Real praise, from a maid. "I do hope she's all right, sir."

"Oh, I'm sure she'll be back after a day or so, she's not badly hurt," Bristow said, glibly. The maid didn't look reassured; but she did seem tired, almost ready to drop. It was half-past twelve, and she'd had quite a day. Should he postpone questioning her? He temporised: "Is there a list of the guests?"

"Oh, yes, Miss Francesca had two copies. She ticked off all the people who accepted, and I expect it will be in her bedroom." That all came out in a breathless hurry. "She has a writing-bureau in there." Cissie led the way into that charming bedroom overlooking the river. "Oo, look, it's right on top!"

The list was written in very neat block capitals, with little red ticks against most of the names. Bristow ran his eye down these, and then suddenly started.

"Did Mr. Mannering come?"

"Oh, yes," breathed the maid, "*he* was here."

Bristow put up a commendable show, but could not hide the fact that the name of Mannering had startled him.

At that moment Bristow looked a tired sixty, with grey

hair, thin, regular features, the short but bristly moustache which would have been silvery but for the yellow stain of nicotine. He lit a cigarette from the stub of another as he smiled at the maid.

"All right, Cissie, you can get off to bed. We'll look after everything, there's no need to worry." He let the girl reach the door, and then called: "Oh, just one little thing. Ever seen this before?"

He held out the diamond.

Cissie's eyes grew positively huge.

"Oo, isn't that *lovely*. Isn't it beaut-i-ful! Oo, I've never seen anything like that in my life."

"You keep away from things like it, too," advised Bristow. "They usually lead to trouble."

Cissie smiled with polite disbelief.

"Nothing else you can think of?" asked Bristow.

"Well, she did get a letter, a special messenger brought it," Cissie said belatedly, "I don't know if she took it with her."

They searched the room, but found no trace of it.

Bristow opened the front door for the girl, who slept out, then went back to Francesca Lisle's bedroom. He looked round, went from there to the hall, and was called by a Yard officer who was looking through the other rooms in the flat.

"Something worth seeing here, sir."

"Is there?" Bristow saw the man at a door—that of Lisle's bedroom. He went in. The carpet was turned back at a far corner, and a floorboard had been taken up and put back untidily.

"Carpet wouldn't lie flat, and that's the reason why," said the Yard man. "Wonder what we've got here."

"I wonder, too." Bristow rubbed his chin, making the grey stubble rasp. "I'd like to know why Mannering was here." He was talking as much to himself as to the detective officer. "Shall I tackle him tonight or leave him until the morning?"

"Pardon, sir?"

"Forget it." Bristow grinned. His expression took ten

years off his age. "Time I retired, I've started talking to myself! Well, now, we want a photograph of the girl and of her father, and while we're here, any dope we can find about him."

"Should say this is the chap, sir. I found this in the girl's bedroom, brought it out because I thought we'd want it." The detective officer produced a folder of wine-red Moroccan leather, opened it, and revealed a picture of a man in the middle-fifties. He had the looks to qualify him for a film star set in romantic mould.

Bristow studied the face.

"All we know is that he didn't turn up tonight, but presumably he telephoned from somewhere near by, and presumably she went off to meet him, in a taxi," Bristow said. "We want that taxi. We want a lot of things." Bristow took the end of the cigarette from his lips, studied it as smoke curled about his stained fingers, and decided: "I'll leave him until the morning."

"The taxi-driver?" asked his man.

"No, Mannering," said Bristow.

5

THE WORRIED YOUNG MAN

JOHN MANNERING knew from the moment of waking when it was a morning for humming *pianissimo* in his bath or under the shower, for being sober if not solemn, and for having an early breakfast and leaving for the shop immediately afterwards. This was one of the penalties of being wedded to genius. Only occasionally, and then when prompted by a chance remark of someone whose opinion he valued, did he realise that his wife was exactly that.

Lorna painted.

Mannering collected and traded in precious stones, *obets d'art*, antiques of a highly specialised kind; they had to be rare.

The only intrusions into this state of connubial bliss were Lorna's exhibitions and his peculiar curiosity allied to a strong sense of what the earnest sometimes called awareness of public duty. More truly, it was a sense of justice which had grown out of resentment at injustice. He enjoyed making mild jokes about it. He enjoyed listening to less mild jokes about himself—such as Simon Lessing's "the most knowledgeable private eye who ever winked at Scotland Yard", which was not original.

The truth was that Mannering lived zestfully, with many likes and a few dislikes, and he concentrated on those things which he liked. These included jewels for their own sake as well as their value, people and puzzles, especially if the puzzles concerned people and jewels.

Lorna also lived zestfully. It was not entirely her fault that she spent so much time painting the portraits of the fashionable. Because people were fashionable, they were not necessarily objectionable. She had many relatives, who enthusiastically recommended her eye for line, likeness, colour and "the spirit of a chap, if you know what I mean"; so she was always very busy.

Whenever she rebelled against this form of daily toil, she downed brush and palette and went out in search of a sitter who could really make her heart beat fast, one whom she longed to capture in paint.

On the morning after the party thrown by Francesca Lisle, Mannering knew that Lorna was in revolt. Reason told him that she had seen someone at the party who had unsettled her. He couldn't imagine whom, and did not ask her. There had been Joy Lessing, an elfin little creature, all gaiety and a kind of radiance—but no, she wasn't Lorna's type of subject. The fat redhead——?' Lorna was withdrawn but polite, floated rather than walked about the flat, and hovered between two worlds. Mechanically she asked if he would be in to lunch, and he said no; mechanically she asked if he would be at the shop all day, and

THE WORRIED YOUNG MAN 37

he said he didn't know; with great preoccupation she kissed him on the right cheek when he left for the shop, a little after nine.

He was there before most of the staff, relaxed, mildly amused, still trying to guess who had transfixed Lorna's artistic eye. Not Francesca herself, or she would have said so weeks ago. The good-looking youngster, Simon Lessing, who had paid such open court to Francesca? Francesca had not shown that she had been really aware of him, except for a few minutes when he had said something to make her blush. Lessing had a quality Mannering recognised; he wasn't just another young man, but a fighter. One or two of the young things talked too shrilly, and hero-worshipped with a curious detachment, reminding him of the Existentialists of the Paris cellars—now happily a dying race.

He gave speculation up.

He parked his black Rolls-Bentley in a bombed-site parking ground at the end of Hart Row, which was a narrow turning off Mayfair's New Bond Street, and wondered, as he wondered often, where he would park the car when rebuilding started here. The bombs had fallen a long time ago, now.

He approached his shop, Quinns, from the opposite side of the road. This was because he still enjoyed pride of possession, and because he liked to see his pride as others saw it. He was never sure whether the single treasure on display in the window would be the one which had been there the previous afternoon; this was in the hands of his manager, a quite remarkable man. This man was remotely associated with European royalty, bred in London's East End, possessed of a passion for precious stones which had once led him to theft and imprisonment. He was now manager of Quinns and in sole charge of display. Occasionally, as a concession, he consulted Mannering about the window; it was never more than a formality.

This jewel of a manager, Larraby, was in the window, leaning forward with his arms outstretched to centre the day's exhibit. It was different from yesterday's; in fact, the whole window had changed overnight. Instead of being lined in its narrow depth with some dark-hued velvet, it was lined with gold brocade, itself beautiful enough to be made into a gown fit for a queen.

Upon this was set a crown of jade, with necklace, earrings, pendant and brooches to match. With unerring instinct, Larraby had chosen the one thing likely to attract the attention of a certain Senhor Fernandes do Costelho, a wealthy Portuguese with one of the finest private collections of jade in the world.

Larraby drew back, judicially. He had curly, iron-grey hair and a face which might have been lifted from a Michelangelo mural. How a man could be nearly sixty and still possess the face of a cherub was Larraby's proud secret.

He glanced up and saw Mannering, and withdrew smilingly. When Mannering reached the shop door, Larraby was opening it.

"Good morning, sir. Do you like the contrast?"

"Perfect, and I like the timing better."

"I have a feeling that the gentleman from Lisbon will be calling," said Larraby, with a serene smile. "I don't think it is quite centred, I wonder if you'll be good enough to indicate any change necessary."

"Go ahead," said Mannering.

He stood outside the single window, the woodwork stained dark brown, with a huge oak beam for a fascia board on which the name was printed in gilt, and in Old English lettering. Larraby fiddled, Mannering signalled, soon the pieces were in perfect alignment. Mannering went inside.

For ten minutes he and Larraby discussed the morning's mail, and Larraby carefully tore off all stamps from letters overseas, and tucked them away for a grandchild now approaching collector's age.

"That's a very fine Japanese specimen," he observed, folding his wallet.

"It would have been better if the writer hadn't wanted something for nothing," Mannering said dryly.

It was an object lesson to see him examining the letters. He began each with a kind of hawk-like eagerness which would be maintained if it were exciting; such as news of a Ming vase or a piece of primitive African bronze, or a rare collection newly on the market.

Ordinary run-of-the-mill letters received a thorough but casual reading. Begging letters, or those from the unreliable or the ill-informed, obviously bored him; and he had an uncanny knack of sensing the true value of a letter from the opening paragraph.

When he dictated, it was into a dictaphone; usually he gave Larraby notes from which to write. No single letter warranted a dictated answer that morning; most of them bored him.

Larraby went into the shop, to see Trevor and two other youthful assistants, over whom he ruled as a priest over his acolytes. All of them had a real feeling for antiques, jewels and odd pieces, but as Mannering listened to Larraby giving instructions about a tiny amulet believed to have been unearthed from the ruins of Pyramids built long before the time of the Pharaohs, he found it easy to smile.

Mannering went back to his office.

The morning newspapers were ready for any caller who had to wait in the shop. He skimmed them through. The finding of a girl, whose initials were F. L., in the river near Waterloo Bridge was in the stop press of three papers and reached the front page of two others, after a hurried squeeze. F. L.: Francesca Lisle? He had seen Francesca gay and happy; but she hadn't been very gay last night. Her father had let her down badly, which was a great pity, because it had been obvious that she was very fond of him. Lisle, Bernard Lisle, didn't appear to be a very sociable animal; he had ducked two invitations to the Green Street flat, and that wasn't exactly customary.

F. L. Odd thing, coincidence. And in one newspaper, she was given fair hair and a white dress.

Larraby looked in. "Those two el Grecos are going out, sir, the van's just arrived."

"Oh, lor'," said Mannering. "Pity. I'll come and attend

the obsequies." He got up and went upstairs to one of the small store-rooms on the next floor up. Hanging on the wall were the two el Grecos, saintly heads in a style which no one in the world could mistake, and as genuine as any hoarded at Toledo or elsewhere in Spain. You either liked or disliked them, but could never deny the genius of their painter.

"I will slip them into their crates," Larraby said.

Mannering left him to it. The crating was simple; just a question of putting the framed pictures in, and bending some metal pieces to fasten the end. Trevor carried one downstairs, Larraby the other. A man from the *Fine Art Carriers* was waiting at the door, and took the crate from Larraby.

He let it slip, and bumped a corner.

Metamorphosis took on its full meaning.

"You clumsy lump of pudding, what the ruddy hell do you think you're doing?" roared Larraby, suddenly not even remotely cherubic. "Give me that picture, I wouldn't trust you with a calendar from Woolworth's." He grabbed the crate and elbowed the carrier's man aside; and so great was his reputation that the man followed meekly, apologising.

Trevor, looking round, winked at Mannering. Trevor knew that Mannering would see the funny side whenever one existed. One could be one's natural self with Mannering, too.

Another man appeared at the door. Mannering would not have seen him at once, if the door hadn't been open. He was tall, young, alert-looking. His brown hair was bare, and as he looked at Larraby and the vanman he smiled appreciation of Larraby's remarkable *argot*. His full lips curved as if smiling came easily. He was dressed in a suit of light-brown serge; well-dressed but not foppishly.

It was Simon Lessing.

Francesca Lisle.

Change the name and not the letter, change for the worse and not for better. Silly doggerel, and why should a doggerel about marriage occur to Mannering when he saw Simon Lessing?

Trevor came hurrying.

"All right," Mannering said, going towards the door, "I'll see him. Simon Lessing, isn't it?"

"Yes," said Lessing. He looked just as wholesome at close quarters. His eyes were greeny-grey, an unusual colour, somehow suggestive of a hot temper. He still smiled, but gave the impression that he was only smiling with his lips. "Nice of you to remember me, but could you spare me a few minutes in private?"

"I think so," Mannering said. "Let's go into my office."

"Thanks. Don't be alarmed," Lessing went on, "I haven't come for a job, a reference, money, guidance or something wholesale—and for that matter," he went on with the smile touching his eyes, "I don't even want Mrs. Mannering to paint my portrait!"

Mannering eyed him up and down.

"Unique," he said, and pushed open the office door. "Won't you sit down?"

Lessing said: "Thanks," and when Mannering looked at him across the bow-shaped Queen Anne desk in the small, narrow office, he looked almost embarrassed, his cheeks were a little flushed, and certainly he was on edge; a young man who would get very intense, was probably strong-willed and almost certainly fiery-tempered. "I don't know why it is, but whenever I want to create a good impression, I let something slip out like that. No insolence meant."

Mannering grinned. "None taken! Perhaps you want some tips on how to win the lady."

It didn't get the expected reaction: a quick grin. He didn't get resentment, either. Lessing gulped, and his uncertain, worried expression returned. He was silent for a few seconds, fidgeting with his hands until Mannering offered him cigarettes.

"No, I don't use them, but—er—would you mind if I smoked a pipe?"

"Carry on."

"Thanks!" That was almost effusive. "Er—you meant Francesca Lisle, of course. Funny you should refer to her. I'm a bit anxious. No right to be, I'm not even sure that there's any cause, but—well, mind if I tell you what's happened?"

Mannering said: "No." In his mind's eye, he was seeing the stop-press notices about a fair-haired girl with the initials F. L. found in the river—no newspaper had said whether she was dead or alive.

"Francesca was very worried last night because her father didn't turn up," Lessing said. "You knew that, of course. I—er—I stayed until after ten, couldn't decently stay any longer. The maid was there, everything seemed all right. But I was uneasy. I suppose—oh, what's the point in trying to fool you, I was looking for an excuse to call Francesca! So I rang her up this morning, ostensibly to ask her if her father had come home. You know—anything to start the ball rolling."

Mannering was very still.

"I know."

"Well, she wasn't there. Hadn't been home all night. The maid answered, a rather excitable creature, you may have noticed her. Named Cissie. She said that the police called last night, and were calling again this morning. Francesca hadn't telephoned to explain, or anything like that. She'd just rushed out after getting a telephone call. The maid thinks it was from Bernard Lisle—that's Francesca's father."

"Yes," said Mannering, "I know." He was lighting a cigarette; Lessing was fiddling with his pipe, but the bowl was empty. "Is that all the maid told you?"

"I'm pretty sure it's all she knew."

"I see," said Mannering. Studying Simon Lessing, he seemed to be challenging the younger man to meet his eyes.

Lessing did. He had a square jaw, looking set now; could he take bad news well? Or news which might be bad? Mannering picked up the *Express*, which had the longest paragraph about the girl F. L., and turned it so that Lessing could read; then ringed the paragraph round in pencil.

Lessing read:

"White cocktail gown—fair-haired—aged about twenty—my God, that's her!" He jumped to his feet, eyes flashing; blazing. "No, look, this isn't possible! Francesca couldn't——" He stopped. Suddenly he was issuing a challenge, seemed to defy Mannering to tell him that Francesca was dead. "You can't think she's dead!"

"I neither think nor know anything yet." Mannering picked up the telephone and dialled a number, looking hard at Lessing as he rang. "I'm calling the *Express*, I know a sub-editor there who'll probably know what the F. L. stands for, and how she is."

Lessing nodded curtly. From this angle, his chin was massive and thrusting.

The *Express* answered, Mannering asked for his man, held on, heard his man's voice.

"Hallo, Dick, John Mannering here. Do you know anything about a young woman, taken out of the river near Waterloo Bridge last night, and——?"

The sub-editor interrupted with a chuckle which gave way to words.

". . . you never lose much time, do you? She's alive and likely to be all right, I gather. Francesca Lisle's the name, it'll be in our later editions, and if there's anything in this for me——"

"Not now," said Mannering. "Anyhow, not yet." He covered the mouthpiece with the palm of his hand and said to Lessing: "It was her, but she's all right." He took his hand away. "What's that, Dick?"

The sub-editor said: "The moment I heard that it was a jewel job, I wagered two to one you'd be sniffing around it. Bill Bristow's in charge, of course, and playing dumb with the Press, so if you can let a few words pass your sealed lips, thanks."

"I'll try," promised Mannering. "Thanks, Dick."

He rang off. Lessing had dropped into his chair, and was sweating; not very much, but enough to have a tiny film of moisture on his forehead. He had lost colour, too. Now he forced a smile, cleared his throat, and would have spoken had the telephone bell not rung.

"Sorry," Mannering said, and lifted the receiver. It was Larraby. "Hallo?"

"I'm sorry to interrupt you," Larraby said, "but Mr. Bristow's here, from Scotland Yard."

6

CONSULTATION WITH AN EXPERT

SUPERINTENDENT WILLIAM BRISTOW, who incidentally was an Officer of the Order of the British Empire, Civil Division, was occasionally seen by his friends as tired, almost peevish and even irascible. They knew him to be haunted by a keen sense of his own limitations. He was probably the only senior officer at New Scotland Yard who was better in achievement than in his assessment of himself.

Seen by strangers, or by anyone at the beginning of a case, Bristow groomed himself to be father confessor and sword of justice in the one spare frame. He dressed well, nearly always in light grey, and liked to wear a Homburg a shade or two darker. He also liked to have a gardenia in his button-hole, and his brown shoes to shine.

When he entered Mannering's office he looked at his best; a spruce five feet eleven. His manner had a confidence that would have seemed like cockiness in a smaller man. It was easy for Simon Lessing not to notice the wrinkles under his eyes, and to be fooled into thinking he was nearer forty than fifty-five.

He was almost hearty.

"Good morning, Mr. Mannering, I hope I'm not disturbing big business." He hardly seemed to glance at Lessing.

"I never have any big business," Mannering said. "I have to slave."

Bristow grinned at Lessing. "Hark at him!"

"Mr. Simon Lessing, Superintendent William Bristow," murmured Mannering. "Mr. Lessing called to see me about Francesca Lisle, Bill."

Bristow couldn't have moved more quickly if he'd been pricked with a pin. Suspicion poured into him; he glanced from one to the other, and finished up by concentrating on Simon Lessing.

"May I ask why?"

"He was worried because Francesca didn't sleep at home last night, and the police had been talking to her maid." Mannering brushed that aside as unimportant. "I take it that you know I was at the party."

Bristow grunted. "Yes. Yes, I know." He wasn't as happy as he had been, but was very much the detective. "What time did you last see Miss Lisle, Mr. Lessing?"

"Just after ten o'clock."

"Can you be more precise?"

"Well—no," said Lessing, and looked awkward. "I know it was about ten. After, because the clock struck in the hall just before I left. A few minutes after ten, say."

"And I left at twenty minutes past eight," Mannering murmured. If the light of battle were in his eyes, it was very dim. "What time was she found?"

"Half-past eleven or so," said Bristow, "she——"

"If you could be more precise——"

Bristow jerked his head up, glared; and then became the man whom Mannering knew well, human, probing, always keeping at his job if not always on top of it. A man who was always trying to do three things at once, quick on the up-take but slowed down by the weight of routine and the difficulties of being a detective.

"Very glad you two were there last night, you may be able to help. Do you know Miss Lisle well, Mr. Lessing?"

"Fairly well, but my sister Joy knows her better."

"Family friend, eh? Do you know Mr. Lisle?"

"I've never met him."

"Mannering?" Bristow switched with a snap.

"No," said Mannering, "Francesca's been to Green Street occasionally, that's all. You've discovered that she has the same obsession as my wife, I imagine." He had a deep voice, a dry way of talking, a quirk at his lips which suggested that it wouldn't take much to make him smile at the follies of the world and of C.I.D. men. "Do you know how she got into the river?"

"Pushed."

"Sure?"

"Yes."

"Pushed!" exclaimed Lessing, and jumped up. "Good God, do you mean someone tried to murder her?"

"Know anyone who might want to?" Bristow flashed.

"Do *I*? Lord, no! Look here——"

"It's all right," Mannering said, "this is simply the Scotland Yard process of riling you. Any idea why it was done, Bill?"

Bristow had taken something out of his waistcoat pocket. It was just a fluffy piece of cotton-wool. He rolled and squashed it between his finger and thumb, glancing at Lessing as he did so. He looked at Lessing for a long time, giving the impression that he wasn't sure what to make of him, nor what question to ask next.

"Did Miss Lisle possess many jewels, d'you know?"

"No idea," Lessing said. He was quieter, and getting over the shock. "No, I don't remember——" He broke off.

Bristow was quick to pounce. "What is it you do remember?"

"As a matter of fact, she was wearing a jewelled cross last night," Lessing said. "It was really something. But Mr. Mannering——"

"See it?" Bristow asked Mannering.

"Yes, Bill."

"Valuable?"

"Very."

"Ever seen this?" Bristow seemed to snap his fingers, and send the cotton-wool floating to the floor. He revealed the round diamond. The beautiful gem did as it would always do where there was light; seized that light, and threw it back in the room a hundred times brighter.

Bristow rolled it along the desk, as he might a marble, and it made a trail like a meteorite touched by a rainbow.

Mannering stopped it.

Bristow was looking at Lessing.

"Mr. Lessing?"

The question was unnecessary, for Lessing's expression made it obvious that the sight of the diamond bewildered him; and it wasn't the bewilderment of a man who had something to hide. There was wonderment, too.

"No," he said slowly. "You mean, have I seen it before? No. Was *that* Francesca's?"

"Ever seen it before, Mannering?" asked Bristow, and settled back in his chair. "That's why I'm here, of course, for expert advice—and I don't know anyone with a greater knowledge of precious stones than you." He almost purred.

"Don't you?" murmured Mannering, in that gently sardonic voice. He opened a middle drawer in the desk and took out a small black case; opened this and showed a pair of tweezers, some needles and a fragile-looking pair of calipers. Then he turned round and took a set of tiny brass scales from the shelf behind him, a set more likely to be found in a scientist's laboratory than in an office.

To Lessing, this was all new ground; to Bristow, it was almost routine; and to them both, it was fascinating. That was due less to anything Mannering did than to his obvious and utter absorption in what he was doing. It was as if only he and the diamond were in the room.

He picked it up in the tweezers and placed it on the scale. The tiny needle of the scale pointed to 4·7 carats. He jotted this down on a note-pad, then placed the diamond on the desk, next measured diameter and circumference with the calipers. All the time, the scintillas of fiery light chased one another in brilliant, changing colours. Still completely absorbed, Mannering switched on an Angle-poise light and swung it round. It did the impossible, and gave the diamond more brilliance. He took a watch-maker's glass from a drawer, screwed it into his right eye with the speed of long practice and, holding the diamond in the tweezers, took his time over inspecting it.

Bristow, obviously used to performances like this, sat and smoked.

Simon Lessing looked and felt bewildered. This wasn't his world. The reassuring thing was the evidence that Mannering knew exactly what he was doing, and that a highly placed Yard official came here for his opinion. It added to the legends he had heard of Mannering, brought the fabulous down to earth.

Mannering dropped the watch-glass and caught it, put the diamond down, and grinned at Lessing.

"It isn't really mumbo-jumbo," he said, "no one waves any wands. Bill, can you reach that book called *Seventeenth-Century Cuttings and Styles*? Thanks." Bristow's chair creaked as he stretched for the book. "I think you'll find this stone was cut by van Heldt, of Amsterdam, I've never seen smaller facets, and he holds the record. If it's his, it's probably listed." He opened the book. There were several pages of very small print, then plate after plate of pictures all of jewels. Most of the plates were coloured.

Lessing watched as Mannering flipped over the pages; he had lean, brown hands, strong-looking, the nails a good filbert shape. He stopped moving at a page in which diamonds were shown against a black background. At a swift glance, Lessing saw other jewels, brooches, rings, pendants, a tiara, a cross. On one side were lists of measurements.

"Ah," said Mannering, and allowed himself a moment's vocal satisfaction. "I think that's it. The Fiora Collection."

Lessing could see that the words held some deep significance; that showed in Mannering's eyes. Bristow grabbed the book, then shot a swift, suspicious glance at Mannering.

"Are you sure?"

"Nearly. See the cross, too. Francesca Lisle wore that last night, or one remarkably like that. True, I didn't recognise it then. Put the main tiara stone—this one—and the cross together, and I don't think it's coincidence."

CONSULTATION WITH AN EXPERT

Bristow was studying the measurements, his cigarette dropping from the corner of his lips, one eye screwed up against the smoke. Lessing sat very still, and Mannering now seemed to be avoiding his eye.

Bristow put the book down.

"So the Fioras have cropped up again," he said, and let smoke trickle down his nostrils. "Now we're really going to be busy. The girl had both these——" Bristow snapped a question at Lessing. "Did she say where she got that cross?"

"Yes, she——" began Lessing; and stopped abruptly. When he flushed, as now, his freckles seemed to grow darker. He didn't avoid Bristow's eye; just stopped speaking. Bristow had plenty of patience, and Lessing's eyes dropped first. He said emphatically: "I don't want to do anything that might make difficulties for Miss Lisle."

"Reasonable enough, but take it from me you won't help her or make her difficulties less by keeping facts from us," Bristow said. "We use facts to prove more facts, not to make difficulties for innocent people. Where did she say she got the jewelled cross?"

Lessing glanced at Mannering, asking a silent: "Shall I?"

Mannering nodded.

"It was her twenty-first birthday yesterday," Lessing said, "and her father gave it to her as a birthday present. He said it was her mother's."

"Oh," said Bristow. "Did he?" He rubbed the side of his nose, then stubbed out his cigarette. His right eye was watering from the smoke. "Well, obviously we're on to something hot. John, were you just social acquaintances of the Lisles, or had you smelt the Fiora trail?"

"As I sit here, I simply thought Francesca a nice girl," Mannering declared. "Lorna thought her a promising painter, and we went to the party because she obviously wanted Lorna to be a lion among the Slade students."

"H'm," said Bristow. "Well, all right—what are you going to do about it?"

"What do you want me to do?"

"I wish I could say, not a damned thing," said Bristow,

with a twisted smile, "but I'd better ask you to see if you can pick up any trace of the rest of the collection. It looks as if they're likely to go the rounds. Better for you to do it than me; if official inquiries are started at once, whoever they are will keep their heads down. Mind if I take the diamond?"

"Welcome," said Mannering, and picked it up in the calipers, put it on a piece of cotton-wool, and handed it to Bristow. "Have you found anything else, Bill?"

They'd started off with some formality; it was now obvious that they were familiars.

"Not much. The girl was pushed in off the Festival Hall Terrace steps. We found a cigarette, plain tip, probably a Virginia One—I'm having paper and tobacco checked. And we found some cotton-wool and got a footprint, size eight shoe, pointed toe, even walker. That's about all." He stood up, slipping the diamond into his pocket. "I'll be grateful for anything you pick up, but be careful—if the original thieves are on this job it could be nasty." He didn't pause, didn't change his expression, but glanced at Lessing. "Any idea where the girl's father is, Mr. Lessing?"

"No. No, I've never even met him."

"Miss Lisle might have said something about him that would give you some idea."

"I think she did mention that he had an office in the City. You could try there."

"Oh, yes, but he hasn't turned up there yet," Bristow said. "Take a piece of advice from me, Mr. Lessing, will you?—hold nothing back. You won't help anyone by hiding facts. Good morning. Be seeing you, John." He turned the handle of the door. "No, don't get up."

He went out.

Lessing said sharply: "We didn't ask where she is!" He jumped up.

"We'll find out, don't chase Bristow now," Mannering advised.

Lessing hesitated, then sat down again.

Mannering picked up a piece of cotton-wool, and began

to mould it in his fingers. Lessing waited until he couldn't wait any longer.

"What's behind this, Mannering? What do you know about those jewels?"

"They were stolen from a London jewel-merchant, three or four years ago," Mannering said quietly. "The merchant was murdered—tortured first, to make him give away the secret of his strong-room, then brutally murdered."

Lessing didn't speak, but lost a little colour as the significance of that dawned on him.

7

A MAN AND HIS FRIENDS

SIMON LESSING could not have behaved better had he set out to make a good impression above everything else. Obviously he saw some of the implications of the news, and didn't like them; but he let them settle in his mind before speaking. All this time, Mannering watched, assessing him with reasonable accuracy. Lessing came from a good family, from Public School but not a university, probably had a little money of his own, and had a mind which might become very good with a few years of experience. That clean-cut look would prejudice most people in his favour; especially Francesca Lisle. He was proving that he could hold his aggressive temperament in check.

"Well, I don't like the look of that much," Lessing said.

"Which aspect of it?" asked Mannering.

"Francesca's father having stolen jewels. But he said——" Lessing broke off.

"The cross belonged to Francesca's mother?"

"Yes." Lessing at last began to fill his pipe. "Francesca—er—positively adored him. You know what I mean.

What a damned awful thing to say to a girl if it wasn't true! And if she finds out that it was stolen——"

"If I know Francesca, she'll flatly refuse to believe it," Mannering said; "we won't lose any sleep about that. She'll have exactly one worry—finding her father. The police will help with that, anyhow, but it may not be so easy, and they may find just his body."

Lessing rammed the tobacco home.

"Yes, I'd thought of that. What an ugly situation! And Francesca won't be in any state to be told about it." He jumped up. "We ought to have asked Bristow how she was, what she knows, what they intend to do with her. She can't go to the flat alone with that addle-pated maid. And who's going to break this news to her?" Once he let himself go about Francesca, Lessing seemed very young indeed.

"One thing at a time," counselled Mannering. "Bristow's a human being, and he won't scare the wits out of her."

"He may think she knows how her father got the jewels. He may try——"

"Of course he'll question her," Mannering interrupted, "but he won't third-degree her, he won't go against medical instructions or do anything which might give her grounds for complaint afterwards. There's nothing we can do about it anyhow, and nothing we ought to try to do— except find out where Francesca is and how she is. That'll come a bit later on. Has she any friends?"

"Only at the Slade. Joy—that's my sister—knows her pretty well. The Slade, home and her father are her only interests. I wonder if——"

"We'll find out where she is and get Joy to go and see her," Mannering said, and that was balm to a troubled young man. "I must get busy too."

"You mean, looking for the rest of the collection?"

"Or listening for rumours about it."

"Why did Bristow come to you?"

Mannering chuckled. He had very white teeth which looked bright because his face was so tanned.

A MAN AND HIS FRIENDS

"I have some queer friends," he said. "Jewellers and antique dealers who sometimes get hold of stuff that I can handle. Usually they offer me only goods they get by honest means, but occasionally they try to pass off something hot. A sale through Quinns puts the price up, you see. Bristow and I work smoothly together."

"You mean, you actually deal with—*crooks*?"

"The odd thing about them is that they're human beings all and crooked only part of the time," said Mannering. "And am I the one to judge? There's a fringe world, Simon. A lot of these people live half in and half out of it, and—oh, never mind."

"The peculiar thing from my point of view is that Bristow knows and seems to approve." Lessing had to make his point.

"I wouldn't say approve. Sometimes he condones! Where can I get you on the telephone?"

"Whitehall 91497," Lessing said. "That's my office— I'm an architect, just set up on my own. Joy and I have a little flat in Knightsbridge." He wasn't thinking about what he was saying. "Mannering."

"Hm-hm?"

"I want to help."

"I don't know that you can," said Mannering bluntly. "There's nothing to stop you from telephoning Scotland Yard, finding out where Francesca is, and arranging to visit her. Why don't you do that and telephone me later in the day?"

After a pause, Lessing said: "Yes, I will, thanks." He didn't try to persuade Mannering to accept his "help". He didn't turn to go, either; there was a look of uncertainty in his eyes. Then words came explosively: "You are a private eye, aren't you? I mean, you do really accept commissions, you don't just help the police as a consultant."

"We have been on opposite sides of the fence," murmured Mannering.

"That's what I mean. But are you committed to Bristow in this case?"

Mannering kept a straight face. "I'm committed to

find out and to tell him if I get any news of the other jewels."

"No further?"

"And I'm expected to pass on any relevant information which might reasonably be expected to help him to find a criminal or criminals."

"Expected?"

"Sooner or later."

"Look here," said Lessing fiercely, "I want to help Francesca, but I don't even know how to begin. Will you help her? Bristow obviously wants to prove that her father's mixed up with crooks, and I'd like to try to prove that he isn't. You'd be working on the same job from a different motive, and I—er—I'd pay any fee, within reason." He coloured, hotly. "I don't want to cheat the law, but——"

"Let's leave all this until we see what happens next," Mannering suggested. "I'm with you part of the way."

"How do you mean?"

"Helping Francesca."

"That's all I want."

"We may not always see eye-to-eye about what is going to help her," Mannering said dryly. "Call me later, Simon, will you?"

"Yes, all right," Lessing said, and turned to the door. Doing so, he caught a glimpse of a portrait on the wall opposite the desk; the portrait of a man who was the spit image of Mannering, but dressed in the fashion of a Regency buck, powdered hair and periwig, scarlet stock, ruffles and red satin coat. Lessing glanced at Mannering, then back at the picture. "Good lord," he said, "that's uncanny!"

"Most natural likeness in the world," Mannering told him. "My wife painted the face from life, and the clothes from a costume piece. She changes the clothes about once a year, the face is paint inlaid in paint."

Lessing went off, chuckling; momentarily lighter-hearted.

. . . . .

A MAN AND HIS FRIENDS

Mannering saw Larraby talking to a short man with very broad shoulders and a completely bald head. He went back into the office, put the calipers, tweezers, scales and watch-glass away, and picked up the little piece of cotton-wool. Then he studied the book. There were seventeen large jewels in the Fiora Collection, and twenty-two small ones. The small ones could never be identified if they were taken from their setting, but unless the larger stones—all diamonds—were cut down, they could be identified against the book's description of the work of the Dutch genius, van Heldt.

Mannering picked up the telephone.

In a few seconds Lorna answered.

"Hallo, my sweet," said Mannering, and made words more than casual endearment. "Bill Bristow's been here, and Francesca's in trouble."

"Oh, John, no!"

"Yes. Someone pushed her in the river. She's all right except for shock—Bristow's having her looked after."

"But why——?"

"That cross her father gave her was stolen," Mannering went on. "A stolen diamond was found on her, too. I'm to probe, which means that I'm in temporary favour at the Yard. Simon Lessing is all emotionally anxious, if he can be believed."

"Any reason to doubt him?" Lorna was quick.

"Every artist loves a nice boy! No. But Lisle didn't come to the party. That might possibly have been to avoid me, or it might have been to avoid one of the other guests. Or for totally different reasons. Busy today?"

"I can see I'm going to be."

Mannering chuckled. "Blessed be those who foresee the future. Go round to Francesca's flat, will you? Tell the maid how sorry you are, is there any way you can help, and with low cunning compile a list of the names of the people at the party. And pump the maid, looking for anything odd or unusual about Bernard Lisle, or odd and sinister or even mildly mysterious callers. You know."

"I'm not a bit sure that I want to play detective," Lorna

said. "I suppose you're going to visit your unsavoury friends?"

"Say that to Simon Lessing, and he'll agree with you warmly!"

"If you really think it will help the girl I'll see what I can do," promised Lorna, with obvious reluctance. "Don't go and do anything silly, we're going to the Plenders to-night."

"These parties——"

"It's their anniversary, and we have to change for dinner. Don't be back a minute after six," Lorna warned.

. . . . .

Mannering went upstairs to a room on the third and top floor, where he kept some clothes. Larraby, the manager, often slept in a small room opposite this. Mannering whistled softly to himself, took off his perfectly cut suit of honey brown, dressed in another, of grey, which fitted where it touched. It had the look of a City man's week-end suit, the knees were baggy, the pockets sagged, the cuffs were beginning to fray. This change alone made a startling difference to his appearance. He could change it a great deal more, but this wasn't an occasion for showing his prowess, only for looking less conspicuous than he would if he wore his usual clothes in the East End. He transferred cigarettes, lighter, wallet, money and all other oddments to the old suit, and went downstairs. Larraby and the bald-headed, broad-shouldered man were still deep in conversation. The stranger was not English.

Trevor, a tall young man in black coat, striped trousers, dark, flat hair and pronounced widow's peak, hastened to open the door for Mannering. "When will you be back, sir?"

"I don't know, Trevor. Hold the fort."

"Don't worry about that, sir."

"Don't worry about that," mused Mannering, and marvelled at the spirit of that young man, who did not look at all like a hero. Six months before, when Mannering had become involved in a case which had started off much less ominously than this one, an assistant at the shop had been murdered. Here was another case with danger obviously in the offing, and Trevor would "hold the fort"! In spite of all the railing at modern young men, there were a lot of Trevors.

And Lessings.

Mannering walked towards the parking lot, passed the Rolls-Bentley, for he no longer looked qualified to sit at the wheel of such opulence, and eventually came to Piccadilly and waited at a bus stop. It was now midday. Piccadilly was crowded, both here and at the Circus a little farther along; ten minutes in that maelstrom and a saint could become a misanthrope. Two small, brassy-haired girls wearing shoes with absurdly high heels eyed Mannering with open admiration, and a tall, classy woman carrying a French poodle pretended that she wasn't. He went to the top deck of a Number 96, found a front seat free, sat down and lit a cigarette. London unfolded in front of him. Scurrying people risking death beneath the wheels of bustling taxis, monstrous buses, perky little private cars. Here and there the black-and-white daubs of zebra crossing held up the impatient, and people walked across these disdainfully; only at such places did they seem to be in no hurry.

Fleet Street was crammed. The crowds thinned at Ludgate Hill, massed again on the step of St. Paul's, where a military band was playing something from Grieg, and where office workers thronged the steps and the space between the pillars, eating sandwiches, listening, smoking. At the Bank traffic and people seemed to be going in three directions at once. Looking down on the narrow confines of the City streets, it was like peering down upon a myriad of Lilliputians.

And someone, a person who had been and almost certainly still was a cypher in London's nine millions, had pushed Francesca Lisle into the river, believing that she would drown.

It would take a hard, ruthless man to kill such beauty.

They were nearing Aldgate. Mannering could see the

old pump at the end of this road, still ready to quench the thirst of parched Londoners as it had been for generations. A few hundred yards along, and the character of London would change. Here in the city there lived, by day, the black-coated barrier between West End and East. Mannering's odd friends lived mostly in the East End. They would probably be glad to see him, although one or two, perhaps with stolen jewels on the premises, would wonder if he were actually on the look-out for those jewels, and would wish him to hell.

These would be the more outwardly overjoyed at meeting him.

Somewhere there lay hidden a clue to the attack on Francesca; to her father's disappearance; and to the murder of a man who had been murdered for the Fiora jewels. The old, dead man had been a friend of Mannering, and he had suffered savagely.

So there were two good reasons for wanting to find a clue; justice and vengeance for an old man, and help for a young girl.

It had been four years or more since the murder, and there had been no clues to the killers until now. It might take another three years to find the next clue; or it might be found this very day.

Mannering climbed down the stairs as a clippie called: "*Allgit.*" He beamed at her, and she rounded her eyes and said: "Ta-ta, sir." He swung on to the pavement, one of the East End crowd, dressed no better and not so well as some of the others, ears quickly tuning themselves to the cries of hawkers, barrow-boys and newsboys. He walked briskly. Across the road, the wholesale butchers were beginning to close their warehouses, but great, raw-looking carcases or mammoth sides of beef hung, dripping. Here kosher and Gentile butcher lived next door to each other, here the masses swarmed, here lay the main hope of finding more about the Fiora jewels.

Mannering made three calls and drew three blanks.

He entered the fourth shop, in a side street near Whitechapel Library, and knew that he had stepped into a place of fear. He was greeted by a frightened man, a little, middle-aged chap, almost a dwarf, with a face which could have qualified him for a clown at any circus. This was a hump-backed, black-eyed dealer in jewels, who had the look of a confirmed rogue.

In a way, he was.

In a way, he was as clean as a policeman's whistle. He gave a square deal, he was a reliable friend to many; even the police liked him, in spite of the fact that they hadn't yet caught him with stolen jewels.

When he recognised Mannering, he actually shivered.

8

A HALF-TALE OF A FRIGHTENED MAN

"HALLO, Prinny," greeted Mannering, and smiled as if in the gloom of the overcrowded shop he hadn't noticed that the proprietor was so frightened. But he was asking himself why, and could not stop his own heart from beating faster. Could this be the luck he needed; to find a clue at the fourth instead of the fortieth visit? "Nice to see you again. And you look as if you're prospering."

He offered his hand.

The man named Prinny took it, gripped nervously with icy fingers, and let it go.

The shop was a junk-heap. On one side, tray after tray of cheap broken jewellery, old watches, clocks, china, hideous brass pieces, knives and forks, all overladen with dirt and dust. On the other was the "furniture". In the middle was a narrow path, covered with a strip of narrow linoleum with its original red-and-brown surface worn off, and at the end of the shop a little counter with a hatch leading to it. Behind the counter was a door to the downstairs room and the stairs to two rooms above.

"Hallo," said Mannering, as if surprised. "Aren't you feeling too good?"

"Good?" echoed Prinny, in a plummy voice. "First I see the Devil himself, and then who do I see? I see the father of the Devil." His voice was a thin wail. "Do me a favour, Mr. Mannering, go away from here, put a notice on the door you won't ever come back. Will you do that jus' to please me?"

Mannering said sympathetically: "You must have had a shock. Which particular Devil came to see you?"

"Mr. Mannering," gabbled Prinny, more plummily than ever, "I don't want to lie to you, I don't want to be bad friends with you. I jus' don't want to see you now. Tomorrow or next week or *last* week, that would be fine, but not now, please. You make me talk, and I don't want to talk. So be a pal, go away, please."

"Who was it, Prinny?"

Prinny wrung his hands.

"Now the limpet has competition, and always it happens on the wrong day! All right, all right, ask me what you want to ask me, and if I want to answer I will answer, and if I don't——"

"Fioras, Prinny?"

"Oh, what have I done to deserve this?" groaned Prinny. "What gets into you, Mr. Mannering? Is it second sight? If you would do me a favour, jus' go away. Have I ever harmed you?"

"So you've been offered some of the Fioras?" Mannering murmured.

Prinny looked appealingly into his face. Prinny's black eyes were shiny, as with tears of pleading. His skin had a yellowy pallor. He was Punchinello without knowing that he could make the world laugh by just being himself. A frightened Punchinello.

"I've just been asking myself, Mr. Mannering, what to do for the best. That's what I've been doing. And I know the answer now, I'll talk to you about it, but heaven help me if anyone finds out. But I know a man I can trust, don't I?" He kept wringing his hands, and the hard skin made a slithering sound. "As God's my judge I'm not wicked, you know that. I never buy a single article knowing it to have blood on it. If I tell a man where he might find a buyer, well, is that so wrong, Mr. Mannering? If I didn't tell him someone would, wouldn't they?" He looked as if he were about to burst into tears. "But he's a clever devil, he——"

Prinny stopped.

He was looking past Mannering towards the door, and something that he saw outside made him stiffen, and cut across his words. Mannering didn't look round. Prinny licked his lips.

Then he seemed to wince.

"Mr. Mannering," he begged, "be a friend, go away, let someone know I didn't tell you a thing, not a thing. Be that kind of a pal, Mr. Mannering."

"All right, Prinny," Mannering said, very mildly, "but don't get yourself into trouble. Bristow is on this job. There was attempted murder last night, more blood on the Fioras. Don't be scared into helping people who might get you hanged."

"Jus' go away," Prinny implored, "that's all I ask."

There was nothing to be gained by staying now. Obviously Prinny had been visited by someone who terrified him, and was in dread lest he should be thought to be making a deal with the owner of Quinns.

So he was probably being watched.

Mannering turned away. To the little dealer, he must have looked enormous. The ill-fitting suit was big across the shoulders, too. He opened the door and went out, nodding to Prinny, who had retired to the doorway behind the counter. Then Mannering turned right, towards Whitechapel Road.

Looking into a newspaper shop next door was a youngish man. Mannering had one swift look at him. He had a sallow, clean-shaven face with a dark dusting of stubble nothing could banish completely, smooth features, a well-cut suit and a new Trilby hat of navy blue. This man didn't look at Mannering. He stared at the magazines and paperback books in the window, and could undoubtedly see Mannering's reflection. Mannering did not give him a second glance, but walked past, taking long strides, making his gait look a little unsteady.

He stopped at the corner. Traffic rumbled by. A cyclist cut in too close to the kerb, and made him dodge back. That gave him an excuse to look round; the well-dressed man had disappeared.

Mannering crossed the road, which was cobbled, very hard on the feet and slippery too. Opposite, there was a public-house, near it a cafe. Big enamel dishes were in the window with sausages, tomatoes, eggs, onions, hamburgers and rice pudding, all cooking—everything but the rice was sizzling in fat. Mannering went in. The smell of frying, hot and choky, struck at him overpoweringly. Farther along, forty or fifty men and a few girls were sitting close together on long benches, hot food in front of them. Nearer the door was a long service counter, opposite it some stools and a shelf. A few people sat here, eating. Mannering ordered sausages and tomatoes, helped himself to a knife and fork, which were spotlessly clean, although bendable without much effort. He squeezed into a place opposite the counter, from where he could see Prinny's shop. It was ten minutes before the good-looking man came out of Prinny's, and by that time Mannering had finished eating.

The man came his way.

Mannering kept where he was. A girl with fluffy hair was between him and the window, so he wasn't likely to be noticed if Prinny's visitor crossed the road here. A small car, a black Austin saloon, slid towards the man, who got in. Mannering could not see the driver. He moved swiftly outside and stared after the car.

"K42AB," he said aloud; and repeated the number, then scribbled it on a small pad which he slipped from his breast pocket.

He looked towards Prinny's. No one was near that shop

or the newsagent's, except a man on the other side of the road, lounging as a bookie's runner might lounge. Mannering didn't get a good look at him, he was too far away, but he carried away a mind picture; including gingery hair.

He moved quickly towards a telephone kiosk, but a man was talking earnestly into the mouthpiece, and holding a copy of the *Evening News* Racing Special up against the box. He might be an age putting on his money; instead, he finished almost at once, and left.

The kiosk smelt of vinegar and fish and chips.

Mannering dialled Quinns; Trevor answered in his best Bond Street manner, Larraby came on the line sounding like an angel.

"Josh," said Mannering briskly, "get hold of a runner who knows his way about the East End, and have him keep tags on Prinny. He's scared and he's being watched, and I'd like to know who by."

"I think I know just the man for the job," Larraby said promptly.

"I don't mean Josh Larraby," remarked Mannering dryly. "Anything turned up?"

"I—ah—have had to change the window," Larraby told him smugly. "Senhor Costelho is leaving London by air tonight, and wanted to take the jade with him. I thought of putting——"

"Congratulations! Fix that runner first and the window afterwards," said Mannering. "Leave it empty if you must. 'Bye, Josh."

He rang off.

No one showed any special interest in him. A policeman, strutting past, obviously remembered his face, but couldn't place him; the man kept looking back. Mannering saluted him with the haste and humility a policeman might have expected from an old lag, and crossed the road to the bus stop. At any other time he might have felt a snug sense of satisfaction, for there were hopes of progress. He felt no satisfaction at all. He didn't like it when the Prinnys of the world were so frightened. He wanted to know why Prinny was scared, and was pondering ways of finding out.

Any thought of telling the police that he'd found a line had died at the sight of Prinny's fear. If he told Bristow, Bristow would have to visit Prinny, and Prinny was already frightened enough. Leave him a little longer, and he would talk. The police would be seen, too. Mannering wished the bus would come. He wondered how Francesca was. He wondered what Simon Lessing was doing, and whether Lessing's interest in the girl was simply romantic. He hoped it was. A bus came up, and two cars passed on the other side of the road, going fast. One was a pale-green Wolseley, and at sight of it Mannering backed away from the bus.

"Make up yer mind," the conductor growled.

"I'll take the next," Mannering said, and dazzled the man with a smile. He didn't feel like dazzling anyone. He watched the green car swing round the corner into the street where Prinny had his shop, and recognised Bristow at the wheel.

He walked past the end of the street.

Yes, there was Bristow's car, outside the shop; and the shabby youth was walking away. Mannering watched him. He crossed to the telephone kiosk at once, and it was empty for him. Mannering reached the pavement by the kiosk as the youth dialled. He was answered almost at once, spoke urgently, and kept looking down the street; so he was probably reporting that the police had called on Prinny.

He mouthed the last word. "Okay." Then he pushed the door open and stepped out.

Mannering moved at the same time, they cannoned into each other, and Mannering trod on the youth's toe hard enough to hurt, then fell heavily against him. Pain stifled anger. The youth snatched his foot from the ground, and kept his mouth wide open in a strangled cry of anguish. People stopped to watch. A girl got off her bike. Mannering was full of apologies—for what he'd done, for being in a hurry.

They parted.

This time, Mannering walked very quickly away from

A HALF-TALE OF A FRIGHTENED MAN 65

the scene, and found a taxi outside Aldgate Tube Station.

"New Bond Street, Oxford Street end," he said, and got in and sat back, breathing more quickly than usual.

The taxi moved off.

First Mannering lit a cigarette, then he took out a yellow pigskin wallet, nearly new, which had been in the youth's pocket a few minutes earlier. The three unpleasant photographs didn't surprise him. Twenty-one pound notes, kept together by a rubber band, didn't really surprise him either; it simply told him that the youth was being paid well to do what he was told. He was gratified by the sight of three letters, all addressed in immature hands to Charlie (one was spelt Chas) Ringall, at the same address in Whitechapel.

The surprising things were the telephone numbers. The Slade School and the Lisles' flat were among several others.

"I think we might get a slice of luck soon," Mannering said aloud. He put everything away, drew hard at his cigarette, and pondered. He was really sorry that Bristow had reached Prinny so quickly. What had brought the police?

The case might break open. If Prinny talked and could help the police, Bristow would get busy in a hurry, and Bristow was as good as the Yard had. It might not be a case for Mannering after all. That would please Lorna.

He bought a newspaper at the corner of Oxford and New Bond Streets. The Press had all the story, and a picture of Francesca on which they'd gone to town; she looked almost as lovely as she was. There was a story of the party, and the fact that Mr. and Mrs. John Mannering had been present was there for all London to read. Mannering was described as the "expert in precious stones and *objets d'art* and famous for his investigations into crimes concerning the loss of jewellery". The Press was a continual thorn in the flesh, but it also traded in roses. At least one Fleet Street man would readily help if help were needed.

Mannering reached the corner of Hart Row. He was not expecting anything unusual. At most, he thought that one or two Fleet Street men would be waiting for him. In fact, there was one. There was also a stranger whom he had seen once before that day; the one who had scared Prinny, and had gone off in a small Austin.

He was just standing, waiting.

9

THE REPRESENTATIVE OF BIG INTERESTS

THE Fleet Street man was curly-haired, bright-eyed Chittering, head bared, raincoat open, shoes in need of cleaning, smile almost as cherubic as Larraby's. Chittering was a friend, a wise man, a good reporter and by no means a bad detective. Most of the mistakes he made were out of ignorance of certain circumstances, and his mistake that afternoon sprang from that cause. It had happened before Mannering could do anything about it.

"Hallo, Private Eye," he greeted, "they tell me you're on the Fiora Collection trail again. What a sleuth!"

The sleek, well-dressed stranger was looking into a window where three hats, all ridiculous, flimsy-looking wisps of millinery, were displayed on long sticks topped with faces which the artist could only have dreamed up after a scarifying nightmare.

"Wrong as usual," Mannering said. "I'm not on any trail."

"Liar. Francesca Lisle, too!"

"Coincidence." Mannering had his back to the stranger now, and winked fiercely. Chittering had the wit not to change his expression. "I've had a rough time at a sale room, Chitty, I need a bath and a change before I feel human again. And I've nothing for you, anyway."

"Keep this up, and you'll almost convince me," Chittering said. "At least tell me this—is it true that Francesca is a pupil of Lorna?"

"No. They happen to like each other. Lorna will help the kid all she can, of course, that's all."

"No inside story," Chittering mourned, and gave a Gallic gesture. "I give up. Let me know if anything should break, won't you?"

"Yes."

"'Bye," said Chittering.

He went off, towards New Bond Street.

Mannering stepped into the shop, turned to close the door, and saw the sleek stranger staring at him from dark, opaque-looking eyes. He felt a breath of disquiet, could imagine that if that man looked at some people, Prinny for instance, he would be frightening.

Trevor was in proud command, two other young assistants were busy. Mannering went upstairs into a small show-room where china was on one side, dominated by three Ming vases, and Roman, Egyptian and Babylonian pottery and metal ornaments on the other. A small window overlooked Hart Row.

The man was walking away.

That was no answer to anything. The man had seen him at Prinny's and seen him here, and knew who he was. He had overheard Chittering's greeting. For the first time Mannering began to wonder whether it had been a mistake. He went up one more flight, washed and changed back into the suit of honey brown. He made notes of the telephone numbers and "Dear Charlie's" address, then put everything he had taken into an envelope and addressed it to Charles Ringall, Esq., and dropped it into the post basket. He stretched out his hand for the telephone, meaning to telephone Lorna, and the bell rang.

"Yes?"

"Will you speak to a Mr. Prinny, sir?"

"*Who?*"

"Prinny. That is what I think the name was——"

"Yes, all right," said Mannering, recovering. "I'll speak to him." He would have been less surprised by a call from the Prime Minister or the Archbishop of York. He heard the clicking of the private exchange plugs, and the young assistant in the shop said:

"You are through."

"Hallo, Prinny," Mannering greeted.

"You and I must have a little talk," a man said. It was not Prinny. He spoke slowly, and his voice had a suave note and an overtone of confidence. "You shouldn't have put the police on to Prinny, that was a mistake. Just keep this between our two selves, and you won't be any worse off. But don't squeal. You understand, don't you?"

"No," said Mannering softly.

"Now don't be silly. I don't want you to get hurt. I don't want a fight with you or anyone else, Mannering. We can do a deal, and you won't suffer. I'll get in touch with you later. *Au revoir.*"

The man rang off.

Mannering put his instrument down slowly. There was likely to be a lot to learn, and he wanted to learn a lot more about the man who had called himself Prinny. It was probably the sleek man, and he held the picture in his mind's eye. A little less than medium height, dressed in smooth-textured clothes, wearing a new navy blue Trilby and very shiny black shoes. He had that powdery blue jaw of the very dark and a smooth skin; the skin of a man who had just come out of a barber's, after all the face treatments the barber could suggest.

Thirty-odd, Mannering guessed; very easy of movement, too.

Here was a growing problem. The man had spoken as if he felt sure that Mannering would do what he was told—as if he believed Mannering would understand him. Why should he think that?

The telephone bell rang again, breaking Mannering's thought.

"Yes," he said cautiously, and found that the line was

still through to the main exchange, no one was at the private one. "This is Mannering of——"

"This is Simon Lessing," that young man said abruptly. He sounded like an officer in command of a hot spot on a nasty day. "I'm coming round to see you at once, you'll stay there, won't you?"

"Don't be too long."

"I'm on my way!"

Too much of that self-assertiveness, Mannering thought, and he would quickly lose patience with Simon Lessing. Then he wondered how far the events of the past hour, especially the unknown's telephone call, had made him cantankerous. He lit a cigarette and chuckled aloud. Then he put his head out of the office and told a tailor's dummy of a junior assistant to go and get him some sandwiches, and closed the door on: "What kind would you like, sir?" The junior ought to know. Ham. Next, he rang the Green Street flat. The maid answered, Lorna had left just after eleven and hadn't come back.

"But she said not to worry, sir."

"Then we can't possibly worry," said Mannering. "Any callers or telephone calls?"

"No, sir."

"Good. Tell Mrs. Mannering that I called, won't you?"

Mannering rang off, musing that willing maids were priceless.

Chittering didn't telephone, although Mannering expected a call. He fell to wondering what had made Simon Lessing sound so peremptory, and how long he would be.

He was still wondering an hour later.

Lessing didn't arrive at all.

. . . . . .

Simon Lessing put a finger between his neck and his collar, and pulled. He felt hot and sticky, and it wasn't because of the weather.

He was in Francesca's flat, and could see through the open door of her bedroom to the river. He didn't notice the bright flickering of the river.

Francesca was all right, in a nursing home near the hospital. He knew that she had made a statement, that the police claimed to be satisfied, and that a doctor had said that she could leave the following day. So far, so good. He'd also seen his sister Joy. Joy had already been to the nursing home, anxious about Francesca. He hadn't been able to settle to work, and had come round to Riverside Walk because it was Francesca's place and he couldn't keep away.

Mannering was obviously interested; as obviously, he wasn't going to call on him for help. He could hardly blame Mannering, but it would not be easy to sit back and await events. Easy? It was impossible! He might find something at Francesca's flat which the police had overlooked. Or Cissie might remember some odd word that would help. At that stage Simon, a little vague about what kind of help he could give Francesca, did not realise that he was suffering from acute frustration.

So he had gone into the flat, where Cissie had talked incessantly. The police had been there for two hours, looked everywhere, even had the carpets up, and then left. She was indignant and a little excited, and bothered by the newspapermen, too, and she had been photographed *three* times, twice when wearing her apron.

The telephone had come to his rescue.

As he rang off after talking to Mannering, he could remember how glad he had been when it rang. Just for a second.

"This is Mr. Bernard Lisle's flat."

A man had asked in a very smooth, even voice: "Who is that speaking, please. Mr. Lisle?"

"No, he's away. My name is Lessing."

"Oh, yes, of course," said the man at the other end of the wire, as if that explained everything perfectly. "Mr. Simon Lessing, isn't it? And you have a pretty sister, now what's her name? Joy." He repeated the name. "Joy, yes. Am I right?"

He was right, but Lessing didn't say so. Fear was a strange thing, and something in this man's voice, in the way he spoke rather than anything he said, brought fear. It was only a flash, and soon gone. It was rather like the feeling when one slipped at the top of a flight of steep stairs and recovered one's balance without falling.

"Supposing I have? What has it to do with you, and who——?"

"Patience, Mr. Lessing," the man said smoothly. "No one's going to get hurt. That is, unless they're very silly. Pretty little Joy doesn't deserve to get hurt, does she? So we mustn't take risks with her."

"What the hell do you mean?"

"A little later, we'll have a talk together—over a drink perhaps," the stranger said. "Until then, *au revoir*." The French phrase came smoothly, wasn't gauchely pronounced as it was so often after a man had been speaking English.

He rang off.

Simon stared at the mouthpiece, then slowly replaced the receiver. The flash of alarm came again, and this time it didn't fade so quickly. It hadn't been an open threat, but was certainly a threat of some kind. And Joy——

He was very fond of Joy. She had the prettiness of healthy nineteen. She was his kid sister. He worried about her if she came home late.

He telephoned Mannering. . . .

He called good-bye to Cissie, and hurried downstairs. He was angry and still scared, and in this mood, determined to tell Mannering that he intended to help, nothing would keep him away. His anger and fear switched from the suave voice to Mannering, who was someone he could think about and who had brushed him off too easily that morning.

His grey Triumph sports car was parked outside the house, which was one of a long terrace. A string of nine barges, pulled by a small tug, went quietly down river. A man turned a corner, and disappeared. Lessing pulled open the door of the car, slid in, slammed the door, took out his key—and saw the marks on the windscreen. They were chalk marks, and not very clear. Lettering, of a kind.

He shifted his position, and was able to make three words out.

Seen Joy lately?

That spasm of alarm, frighteningly familiar now, came again. This time, its passing left his heart banging with heavy, choking thumps. He didn't begin to ask himself why this was happening; he hadn't had time to be dispassionate. Francesca had nearly been murdered, and now there was this threat.

Of course it was a threat!

He put his foot down hard on the accelerator. The Embankment was clear at this end, and it took him only fifteen minutes to get to the Slade. Several students, two of whom he knew, were coming out of the front door. They stared at him curiously as he hurried in. Obviously he'd come at a good time, students were on the move. He saw the red-haired girl of the party ludicrously filling a thick woollen sweater.

Her eyes lit up.

"Hi, Si!" She broke away from two friends, and approached him. "What went wrong after we left you behind last night, villain?"

"Sue, don't fool. Where's Joy?"

"How should I know? What *did* happen, darling?" She clutched his arm. She was too fat nearly everywhere, but seemed completely free from self-consciousness. She pressed against him. She had a witch's face, sharp nose, green eyes, big red mouth and white but widely-spaced teeth. She screwed her neck to look up at him. "It wasn't you, was it?"

"Sue, where's Joy?"

"Don't 'oo love ickle Susan any more?"

"For Pete's sake stop fooling!"

"My, you are edgy," Susan said, changing her tone. "Don't know, Si. We were sketching glamorous female torsos, and I think Old Seymour came in and spoke to her, and she went out. *Girls!*" Susan swung round suddenly, raising her voice to a strident scream. Everyone within earshot stopped and looked at her. "Anyone know where Joy Lessing went?" she asked, now in a cooing voice.

A sleek-haired youth said: "Her brother telephoned, and she went off to see him. Family trouble, or something urgent."

Simon Lessing heard that, and felt sick.

The red-head looked at him, her expression quite serious now. The light faded from her green eyes, and she looked less like a witch.

"Didn't you call her, Si?"

"No, I did not."

"Then she must have a boy friend. Pretty girls often have boy friends and fix clandestine meetings. Don't worry."

Mechanically he said: "No." He turned and hurried out. Susan watched him, then shrugged her shoulders and joined her companions.

Simon Lessing turned into the street, hurried towards his car, and saw something which jolted him out of his mood.

A man sat at the wheel.

10

THE WHISPER OF SUSPICION

SIMON LESSING did not realise it, but he did not know himself. Present him with an emergency and he acted swiftly, effectively and with judgment. Give him time to think, and he dithered. The news about Joy had frightened him, and overlaying the fear was anger. The sight of the man in his car touched that anger into action.

The man was a stranger, young, dressed in shapeless brown tweeds, in need of a hair-cut; it was affected poverty, there was something arty about him. The long hair was reddish. He looked sideways at Simon with a smooth, sneery grin as Simon slid into the car. He didn't grin for long. Alarm displaced derision, and he flung up a hand and backed against the door. It was like trying to stop a charging rhino. In the confined front seats of the car, Simon smashed at his jaw and at his stomach, hooking and upper-cutting savagely.

The stranger's teeth cracked together. Blood sprang to the side of his mouth and trickled down. Fear burned in his eyes.

Then Simon stopped hitting him.

The car was filled with the gusty breathing of the two men. People passed, students, office-workers, a policeman —footsteps clattered or thudded, legs passed in their line of vision, nice shapely legs, trousered legs—and just legs.

The long-haired youth was shaky with fear; Simon as shaky with tension.

Simon spoke first. "Do you know anything about my sister?" The words were growled, his clenched fists were close to the other's face. "Come on, let's have it."

The youth spat: "You try that again, and you'll never——"

Simon didn't give him a chance to finish. He squealed and thrust both hands up, but couldn't save himself. Simon's hands closed round his throat and squeezed. The man's body heaved and writhed, he clawed at Simon's wrists, his long nails tore the flesh, but he couldn't get himself free. His eyes seemed to be getting bigger and standing out from his head, his lips were parted in a funny kind of snarl.

The car door opened, and a girl said:

"Si, you crazy fool!"

It was Susan; Susan Pengelly. She slapped the back of Simon's head, and the blow made him relax. Then she tugged his hands away from the thin neck. The youth leaned back in his seat, mouth open and eyes nearly closed, a glazed look in those eyes. He seemed hardly to be breathing.

"What do you want, to be hanged for murder?" Susan breathed. "Oh, I'd like to wring your neck! Do you carry a brandy flask?"

Simon gulped. "Er—no."

"Get out and let me get in," she said, "let me see if I can bring him round."

The youth was grunting, in a staggered kind of way.

Simon got out. A gust of wind off the river stung his forehead and neck. He didn't notice anyone in the street. Susan squeezed into his place; he didn't notice that then, either, but she had very nice legs, quite out of proportion to the rest of her body; her hands were small and shapely, too. She slammed the door. Simon eased his collar, wiped his forehead, but had to wait; it was only a two-seater. A young man who had been at the party last night passed in a hurry, and the usual greeting:

" Hi, Si!"

"Hallo, there."

There had been the smooth-voiced man with his veiled threats; then the discovery that Joy had been called away by someone who had said he was her brother. Had Joy really been fooled? Where was Joy? There was the man he had attacked, and who might have some information. The stirring of annoyance with Susan made him bend down and look inside.

She was slapping the youth's face, sharply.

Simon opened the door.

"Move up," he said.

"Si——"

"Move up!"

"Oh, all right, but there isn't really room." Susan squeezed against the youth. His eyes were wide open now, and something of the glazed look had gone. Colour was back in his cheeks. He realised that the girl was pressing tightly against him, and looked at her. He caught sight of Simon, and jerked his head back, gabbling:

"N-n-n-no!"

"He won't hurt you any more," Susan said.

"Won't I?" muttered Simon.

"For the love of Mike have some sense!" The girl's green eyes flamed. "What's all this about, anyway? I wanted to ask if I could help, saw this man sitting here, and——" She didn't finish.

"He——" began Simon, and then braced himself. "He knows where Joy is, and if he doesn't tell me, I'll break his neck."

"I don't think I understand," Susan said. "You sound as if Joy had been kidnapped."

"That's about it."

"Sometimes," said Susan, "I wonder if you're worth all the affection I waste on you. You must be crazy."

"He's crazy all right." The youth was coming back in circulation. He was sweating, and poking his long fingers through his hair. He kept licking his lips and darting sideways glances at Simon. "I only want to make him see sense."

"What about?" Susan asked.

"Sue," said Simon with great determination, "I'm going to handle this." But she was sandwiched between him and the youth, it wouldn't be easy to scare the youth again so easily. "It's not your business, you keep out of trouble."

"I'm keeping *you* out of trouble."

"Listen," said the youth, "your sister will be all right if you behave yourself. No one's going to hurt her. Just get this into your head—Mannering's using you. He's got the sparklers, and we want to know where. Up to you to find out, see? You're a buddy of his, he'll tell you, and you'll tell us. Get me?"

His careless talk wasn't a natural argot; everything about him was phoney, except the swelling on his jaw, his mouth and right eye—and the trickle of blood, which had almost dried up now.

"Gosh!" exclaimed Susan, "you were right!"

The youth raised clenched hands.

"Keep back!" His eyes glittered, as much with fresh fear as with rage. "Listen, Dumpy, you keep his hands off me! So Sister Joy's a guest of someone she doesn't know for a day or two. She'll be well fed, have nice comfy bed, cheerful company, all that kind of thing. But you find out where Mannering's got those jewels. And don't pretend you don't know what I'm talking about, I'm talking about the Fiora Collection. Get me?"

"I *must* be dreaming." Susan gulped.

"No one's dreaming. Don't want your kid sister's pretty face to be spoiled, Lessing? Or do you?"

That sent a quiver of horror through Simon Lessing, and silenced the girl. She didn't know what to say or where to look, while Simon sat cold, limp and frightened.

The youth chose his moment well. He drove a clenched fist into Simon's face, then shoved Susan heavily, banging the top of her head against Simon's chin. He squirmed round, opened the door and jumped out.

A car horn screamed.

The youth cried out, and pressed back against the car, terror-stricken. A taxi passed within an inch of him. As it went, he jumped forward, slammed the door behind him, and leapt towards the opposite pavement. He turned left, towards Fleet Street. Soon he was lost among great lorries with huge rolls of newsprint, among newspaper vans, among workmen. A few watched him running, but no one made any attempt to stop him.

He slowed down when he passed the main entrance to the *Record* building. No one was following him.

. . . . .

Susan Pengelly and Simon sat in the Triumph, both breathing tautly, Simon through distended nostrils, Sue unashamedly through her wide-open mouth. She had stopped rubbing her head. Simon's nose was bleeding, and he kept dabbing at it with a handkerchief which was already crimson.

"That'll teach me," breathed Sue. "I thought you were just having a row. Si, you've got to tell the police."

He didn't answer.

"You've just got to!"

He took the handkerchief away. "I don't know whether I ought to or not," he muttered. "I don't know what to do for the best. Can there be any truth——" He broke off.

"Truth about what?"

"Mannering——"

"Look here," said Susan, "I don't know a thing about this. Oh, I know Mannering was the lion at the party last night, but where does he come into it? Let's drive round to my place, and you can sit back and relax and tell—*Dumpy*," she breathed. "Next time you needn't break that lout's neck, *I* will. Come on."

"I'm not sure——"

"If you don't drive I will, and you'll have a crumpled wing before you know where you are."

"Oh, all right," Simon gave way. "The thing is, if that devil really has kidnapped Joy——" He broke off, started the engine, and let in the clutch. "It's like something in a film!"

"I think the first thing you have to do is make sure that Joy is really in trouble," said Susan, more reasonably. "After all, we've only his word for it. Let's go to your flat, instead of mine."

Simon had already started off.

"Yours is nearer," he said. "We can telephone her."

Susan Pengelly had a one-room-plus-kitchen-and-bathroom flat in an old building near Covent Garden Market. It was reached by a flight of narrow, creaking stairs, but the room itself was very big and had good views over roofs and shops. A big, double-size divan was in one corner, with a wardrobe and chest of drawers; a screen of astounding design and vivid colouring concealed part of this. She had daubed vivid colours on with a careless effect which startled everyone who saw it for the first time. Round the walls were sketches and paintings, all of heads; heads of native Africans, Indians, whites, Maoris, aborigines; the handsome and the ugly. All were from life—all were touched with a kind of malice.

There were easy-chairs, everything comfort demanded.

"Sit down and I'll put the kettle on, we'll have a cuppa," said Susan.

"I'm going to telephone!"

"Oh, yes, of course. Help yourself." She waved to a small desk in a corner, beneath a light which could be raised or lowered, as one wanted. Canvases, some clean, some already daubed or used for sketching, leaned against the wall. One was on an easel. The telephone was on the desk.

Simon dialled his flat number.

There was no answer.

He rang off, dialled two of Joy's friends, and was told the same story; she had left the Slade, soon after lunch, saying that he had telephoned to say there was some family trouble.

By the time Simon had finished, Susan came in from the kitchen with a tea-tray. She put it on a low table, and stood in front of him, arms akimbo. She had rolled up the sleeves of her thick yellow jumper, which fitted her figure so tightly that in places she looked likely to burst through.

She put her head on one side, and had her legs slightly apart.

"Now, give."

"I'm so worried I don't know whether I'm on my head or my heels." Simon jumped up. "You know what happened last night, about Francesca . . . ?"

The telling of everything else took five minutes. Then Susan poured out tea. Between sips, Simon added little touches to the interview with Bristow, the fact that Bristow obviously trusted Mannering, the fact that the dealer who had owned the Fiora jewels had been questioned.

"Mannering *can't* have them!" he burst out.

Susan said: "Can't he?"

"It stands to reason."

"I don't know what you think," said Susan, "but I think that lout this afternoon knew what he was talking about. He knows a thing or two. If Mannering——"

"The very idea's ludicrous."

"You aren't very receptive to new ideas, are you?" asked Susan. "I don't know this Mannering, except that he's a handsome beast, and I'm not prejudiced one way or the other because of his reputation. All I'm worried about is Joy." She shifted her position suddenly, and looked away from him. "And that's a lie," she added, with mock shrillness. "I'm more worried about you. Unrequited lover, that's me. What with Francesca and Joy and me you do have a lot of woman trouble, don't you? Perhaps I'll be more help than hindrance, after all, I did save you from a charge of assault. What are you going to do? I would tell the police."

Simon said: "I suppose I could tell Bristow, but——"

The telephone bell rang.

At the first ting of the bell Simon was out of his chair. He grabbed his cup, to save it from falling, and rushed to the telephone. He didn't even say: "That might be Joy," but rushed, snatched up the receiver.

"*Hallo?*"

There was a moment's pause; then his manner altered, he sagged for a moment, gritted his teeth, and then banged down the receiver. When he turned to face her, he was five feet ten of sagging dejection.

"Was it—them?" Susan asked, in a husky voice.

"They've—they've warned me not to go to the police if I want to see Joy again," Simon said.

11

MANNERING GETS HOME LATE

At half-past five that afternoon Mannering sat in front of the page which illustrated the Fiora Collection, and also in front of his diary. The diary had an emphatic note: 7.30 Dinner at T. P.'s. T. P. stood for Toby Plender. Plender was a barrister of repute, ten years older than Mannering, a close family friend and a man to like. The party was to

MANNERING GETS HOME LATE

do with that very important wedding anniversary, the kind of occasion that made Mannering look at the few silver streaks in his own hair.

It had been a frustrating afternoon.

He had been out for an hour, visiting Francesca Lisle in the nursing home near Westminster Hospital. She had been sleeping, and except that he was told that she was much better and likely to be out tomorrow, it had been a wasted journey.

Lorna had telephoned, to say that she'd a list of some of the people who'd been at the cocktail party, but didn't think it would help.

No one else had called or telephoned. Silence from Chittering; Simon Lessing; Bristow; Prinny. In fact, everywhere was silent as a desert by night. He had telephoned Lessing's home and office, without getting the young man. He had called the *Record*, but Chittering hadn't been there. Larraby had nothing to report from Aldgate or Whitechapel, except that Prinny had been taken to Scotland Yard.

The one cheering piece of news had been that Francesca would probably be able to leave soon.

Where would she go?

The Lessings' flat?

Mannering stood up. Lorna would expect him on the dot of six, and he couldn't blame her. He would be preoccupied at the Plenders', but would undoubtedly be forgiven. He could have calls put through from the office and the flat to the Plenders'. Lorna would complain but accept it. Lorna——

The telephone bell rang.

"That's wonderful," he said, "it'll begin now that I ought to be on my way." He lifted the instrument.

"Mr. Chittering has called, sir," Trevor said.

"John," said Chittering of the *Record*, as he came briskly into the office. "You are a double-dyed villain."

"Why sound surprised?" asked Mannering. "Chair?"

"Thanks. A treble-dyed rogue of the nastiest kind."

"Have you been talking to Bill Bristow? Cigarette."

"Good idea. No. A man named Ephraim Scoby."
"Ephraim?"
"Scoby. At least, that's the name he gave me at his hotel, and it sounds too unreal to be false. How well do you know him?"
"I don't think I do."
"He was outside Quinns this afternoon when you told me in that heavy-handed way of yours to make myself scarce."
"You mean——" began Mannering, and chuckled. "So you followed him. Where?"
"All over London. At first I don't think he knew he was being followed, but afterwards I came to the conclusion that he did, and was enjoying it. Finally, he invited me to have a drink. I've just left him."
"Has there been time for it to act?" asked Mannering.
Chittering sounded blank. "For what to act?"
"The poison."
"You misjudge Citizen Ephraim Scoby. He is the whitest of white sheep, the pure young man who would not tell a lie, do a dirty trick, cheat, defraud or otherwise be illegal. He only wants to make sure that others get their rights. I know all this," added Chittering, "because he told me so. Earnestly."
"He sounds untouchable."
"He's in very great trouble—emotional and ethical trouble, you understand."
"Good."
"He doesn't want to tell the police that you have the Fiora Collection," announced Chittering.
He didn't smile. He didn't play with his cigarette, his hair or anything on the desk. He just sat there without expression, and his clear blue eyes, childish in their directness, were upon Mannering. It was a shock to Mannering, and it took him several seconds to adjust himself to the swing of events. At last he said:
"What a villain I am. And I hadn't realised it."
"Got 'em, John?"
"No."

"Not holding them for the rightful owner and drawing the crooks' fire, are you?"

"No."

"I hope I can believe you." Chittering relaxed. "Between you and me, I don't care for this Scoby chap much. He is the ultra-smooth kind. He has it all under control. He doesn't threaten, just says what a pity it all is and hopes that you won't live to regret holding those jewels. He says he is quite sure that you have them, and he seems to mean what he says. In fact," added Chittering with a grin which made him look positively angelic, "he appealed to me, as a gentleman and a friend of yours, to persuade you to deal with him. After all, he said, no one would want you or your reputation to suffer."

"He's not bad at all, is he?" murmured Mannering; but he looked worried. "I wonder who gave him the idea that I had the jewels."

"He didn't give me a clue. He did say one thing that got under my skin, John. You know how it is." Chittering helped himself to another cigarette from a box which Mannering pushed towards him. He became very serious. "Thanks. A lot of verbiage rolls off one. This man is economical in what he says, and I always had a feeling that there was something more behind it. The thing he said was this: 'Francesca Lisle was lucky, but not every girl in the case can be sure of the same luck.'"

Chittering paused, then struck a match; the sound and the flame added a stab of menace to the words.

"Where did you have this heart-to-heart talk?" Mannering asked.

"In his hotel room—he's at Bowing's. He's been there for two days, hasn't stayed at the place before, and is booked until the end of the week."

"Thanks. He put himself in your hands pretty meekly, didn't he?"

"We mentioned that," murmured Chittering. "He said that hearsay isn't evidence, that he'd deny everything, that he'd found out I was a good friend of yours and wouldn't want you hurt. He took a chance, knowingly. If you ask me, he'll cut and run at the first sign of police trouble. That's beside the point," Chittering went on. "What will you do?"

Mannering's lips began their upward curve.

"Hadn't I better pay him a visit?"

"John," advised Chittering, with great deliberation, "be careful with Mr. Ephraim Scoby. He is dangerous, like a snake. Whether you have these Fioras or whether you haven't, I think he really believes you have."

"I'll be very careful," promised Mannering, "but someone has to disillusion him." He glanced at his watch. "I must go, Lorna will have my neck if I'm not home by six. We're due at——"

The telephone bell rang. Mannering hesitated and scowled at it, and then lifted it. Chittering didn't get up.

"Yes?"

"It's Trevor again, sir, sorry to interrupt you," said Trevor, who always lacked confidence on the telephone, "but there is a young—ah—lady here, who says that she must see you. She says——"

"Tell her I'm sorry," Mannering said, "and that I'll gladly see her in the morning. I must go home now, I've an urgent appointment." He rang off before Trevor could speak again, and got up. "If it's important to her, she'll stay and we'll see her as we go out. Talked to the Yard lately, Chitty?"

"No. Should I?"

"They picked up Abe Prinny at his shop at lunch-time, and he was still at the Yard at four o'clock. I don't want to ask any favours of Bill Bristow, but I'd like to know if they're holding Abe, and why."

"Oke. Where shall I ring you?"

"At the flat or at Plender's."

"I shall probably call in person at Plender's," Chittering said, "he has a cellar which makes yours look like a leaky barrel."

He opened the office door.

Mannering took his hat off a peg, and went out. Trevor was hovering near.

"Sorry it's late, Trevor, but I must rush. Mr. Larraby isn't back yet, is he?"

"No, sir."

"Well, lock up, set the alarms, and then get off. Oh—telephone my wife and tell her I'm on the way, will you?"

"At once, sir," promised Trevor. Far from being oppressed by staying later than usual, he was obviously glad to be entrusted with the task of locking up half a million pounds or so. He was conscientious to a degree, too. He followed Mannering and Chittering to the door, and Mannering asked: "What did the girl say?"

"She didn't say anything, just turned and went out," said Trevor. "I can't imagine it was anything very important."

"That's fine," said Mannering.

The worst of London's rush hour was over. Only a few cars were left in the bombed-site car park. Chittering, having refused a lift, had walked towards New Bond Street. Mannering opened the door of his car, and had a shock. It was a real shock, for he had actually turned the key in the lock—yet a man was sitting in the seat next to the driver's. The light in the car was poor, but the man looked young and slim. Certainly he was ragged-looking, he needed a hair-cut, and he seemed young.

He was nursing a shiny, black-leather cosh.

It was made of pliable leather filled with lead-shot, guaranteed to kill if brought down heavily on the right spot; and capable of knocking out a man with the hardest skull, yet showing little in the way of a bruise. He held it in his left hand, and sat close against the door—as far as he could be away from Mannering.

Nervously?

Mannering hesitated, then slid into his seat. He turned the key in the ignition, started the engine, and let it warm up. He didn't look at the youth or show any sign that he knew he was there. A car in front of his moved off, and he followed. Soon he was driving along narrow streets towards Piccadilly. Out here, the light was better, and sideways glances showed him the reddish hair, the silky stubble and the funny mouth.

Mannering turned into Piccadilly.

"Where can I drop you?" he asked.

The youth seemed to relax. He was grinning, but his hold on the cosh was still tight.

"I will say this for you," he said, "you're a cool card. You can drop me where you like, Mannering, and——"

"When you speak to me," said Mannering, in a voice which had the cutting edge of a carving knife, "you will say 'Mr. Mannering' or 'sir'." He slid the car into the kerb. "Get out."

"Now look here——"

"I said get out."

The youth moved the cosh and shifted his position so that he could use it. He looked half-scared, in spite of his weapon. He had a bruised chin, mouth and eye, as if he had been in a fight quite recently; his mouth looked particularly sore.

"Don't you be so cocky," he shrilled. "You'll get what's coming to you. What's your price?"

"I told you to get out," Mannering said softly.

"You keep still," the youth ordered. "If I swipe you with this, it'll break your jaw. You know what I'm talking about. What's your price?"

Mannering didn't speak, but looked at him levelly—and then gave him a sharp side-kick on the ankle. It hurt. Mannering grabbed a bony wrist, wrenched the cosh away, and brought it down sharply on the back of the youth's head. The first blow was glancing and didn't knock him out, but it scared him. Mannering grabbed his shoulder, pushed him round and struck again.

"*Gug-gug-gug*," gasped the youth, and slumped back in his seat.

Mannering took out a whisky flask, poured some of this over the youth's face, then turned the next corner, made a detour, and soon crossed Piccadilly. Not far from Dover Street Station there was a large hotel in a quiet square, an old-fashioned place, with much dark oak, red plush and brass which needed cleaning every morning. This was Bowing's. A grey-clad commissionaire in a cockaded tip hat and a long coat and many medals, came to open the door.

"Thanks," said Mannering, and smiled his brightest. "Hallo, Fred. Help me out with this chap, will you?" He put the cosh into the youth's pocket, and opened the other door; the commissionaire, in tribute to his training and his self-control, said nothing. The smell of whisky was enough to make the average drinker thirsty.

They dragged the youth out.

"He is a friend of Mr. Ephraim Scoby, who is staying here," said Mannering. "Deliver him with my compliments, will you?"

"I *will*, Mr. Mannering."

"Thanks," said Mannering, and two half-crowns changed hands. Another commissionaire arrived, to help out, and Mannering drove off.

He had not yet decided whether Ephraim Scoby believed he, Mannering, had the Fioras, or whether for some reason he wanted to persuade others that he had. At the moment, that was immaterial. What mattered was getting to the Chelsea flat; he would arrive at least half an hour late. Lorna would be harassed and on edge, and he couldn't blame her. Lorna was a slave to punctuality; if there were a good fault, that was it.

Mannering had made up five minutes of the lost time when he turned into Green Street. He left the car outside the house, and hurried up the stairs two at a time. His flat was on the third and top floor, with Lorna's attic studio above it.

The only way up was to walk.

He let himself in with a key.

"I think this will be him," Lorna said to someone out of sight, and came into the hall. She didn't look harassed, annoyed, reproving or dismayed. "Darling, Miss Pengelly has called and is very anxious to see you. You remember, she was at the party last night. " Lorna's tone and her expression told him that however much she regretted it, she knew that he ought to see Miss Pengelly, whom he did not remember from Adam. Or Eve. "She called at the shop, but you were in a hurry to get home."

"Oh," said Mannering, blankly. He approached the study door, which was ajar. Lorna was close to his side, and whispered: "It's about Francesca, but don't trust her an inch."

"You see how dutiful I try to be," Mannering added, and went into the study, a step behind Lorna.

It was the red-head with the enormous bust, the jade green eyes, the big mouth, pointed nose and sharp chin. She looked as if she had been squeezed and pushed into her yellow jumper as she sat in an armchair, head back, eyes narrowed so that they glinted brightly. She looked like a witch; or a woman who would sit and knit and gossip and laugh with glee while watching heads fell from the guillotine or bodies swinging from the gallows at Tower Hill.

Mannering's greeting could not have been nicer had she been a beauty queen.

"Hallo, Miss Pengelly, I hope you've forgiven me. How can I help you?"

She kept him waiting for an answer. He didn't force her, and Lorna also kept quiet.

"You can exchange the jewels for Joy Lessing," she said at last.

12

MANNERING MISSES A PARTY

MANNERING did not respond to the shock of the challenge. Susan Pengelly was watching him with at least as much intentness as he was watching her. Bad she might be, even the Jezebel that she looked; but she wasn't a fool, and she had said that with calculated purpose.

MANNERING MISSES A PARTY

Lorna glanced at Mannering.

"Don't tell me that you also come from Mr. Ephraim Scoby," murmured Mannering. He moved away, still looking at her, until he reached a cocktail cabinet which fitted into a corner and was disguised as a fourteenth-century cupboard. "Can I get you a drink?"

"Thanks. A gin-and-Italian, please."

"And you, darling?"

"I won't have one now," Lorna said. She was still badly shaken. "You know we mustn't be too long."

"Oh, yes." Mannering poured out the gin, then added Italian vermouth from a bottle with a gaudy label, then a whisky-and-soda for himself. He handed the girl her drink. "Cheers."

"Here's to honest men," said Susan, and tipped her drink down. "What name did you say?"

"Ephraim Scoby."

"He sounds like something out of Dickens."

"He comes from a far, far more unsavoury spot. Who gave you the idea that I have whatever jewels you're talking about? What jewels are they, by the way?"

"You're not bad at dissimulating, are you? I think he said the Fiora Collection."

"Who said?"

"The lout who told me that you had them," answered the girl, and sipped her drink again. "He also said that he had kidnapped Joy Lessing, Simon's sister, and would release her if Simon found out where you kept the jewels. But I don't want Simon getting into trouble, with you or with anyone else. He's in enough trouble over Francesca, she's nearly driving him mad. That girl has a darling-daddy complex."

"Where do you come in?" Mannering asked mildly.

"I'm just the doormat."

"I'd like to know which door."

For the first time, Susan Pengelly laughed. She uncrossed her shapely legs; she took small shoes, and had the trimmest of ankles. Sitting in the chair, she looked as big round as she was high.

"I don't think it matters, but I'm Simon's faithful slave. I've been in love with the hero for years. Unrequited, but I'm the maternal rather than the hot-blooded type, in spite of my over-development. This is exactly what happened."

She had a way with words, and when she described what had happened in the car, it was easy to forget her appearance and the glitter in her green eyes. She made it all very vivid, and succeeded in portraying Simon Lessing accurately—first his furious attack and then his dithering. All this time, Lorna sat on a high stool, *circa* 1500, and watched her. Mannering knew that she should be worried about him changing his clothes, but somehow she wasn't. There was a curious intentness about the way she looked at the Pengelly girl.

Susan Pengelly finished, saying: "And he just ran, leaving you with your reputation besmirched, Mr. Mannering. Simon cries hoarsely that you couldn't do such a thing, but he was always inclined to be a hero-worshipper. Would you credit your husband with such villainy, Mrs. Mannering?"

"The very idea is absurd," Lorna said mechanically.

"What I'm afraid of is that Simon will get himself into more trouble over this," observed Susan. "I saw the way that lout looked at him. If he met Simon in a dark alley, I feel sure he would use a knife or a razor, and Si's far too good-looking to have his face spoiled. But he's desperately fond of Joy, and *in loco parentis*, so to speak. Their parents died three years ago, went down together in a ship, and Simon is guardian and mother and father rolled into one. He takes that kind of thing very seriously. Now he doesn't know whether to storm in here and make you talk or go to the police, or try to look for Joy himself." She paused, finished her drink, and took a cigarette from the box by her side. She lit it, then looked at Mannering through a little haze of smoke. "I'd like to find Joy, too. Have you the diamonds?"

Mannering said: "No." He didn't move, and watched her very closely. "What was this youth like?"

She twisted round in her chair, dug down by the side,

and drew out a large envelope, stiffened with board on one side. She held it out, quickly, screwing her eyes up against the smoke which she had driven into them.

"I got a good look at him," she said.

Mannering opened the envelope, and Lorna left the stool *circa* 1500 to look over his shoulder. It was a quite startling likeness; a camera could have done little better. In fact, the colouring—it was in coloured crayons—improved on any camera. There was the half-sneering, half-furtive look, the parted lips showing the teeth set in a small upper jaw, the reddish hair and reddish shadowing on cheeks and jaw.

The youth's split lips showed; and a trickle of blood reaching his chin.

Suddenly, explosively, Mannering laughed.

Lorna looked at him sharply; Susan wriggled forward in her chair and got up. She didn't reach Mannering's shoulder.

"So it's funny."

Laughter shook in Mannering's voice.

"It's brilliant, you'll make my wife envious! The funny thing is Charlie Ringall's face. Did Simon do this to him?"

"I think he would have killed him."

Mannering sobered. "So he reacts like that, does he?" He held the drawing away from him, for better effect. "Poor 'dear Chas.' He——"

"Are you saying that you know him?" asked Lorna incredulously.

"We've met," said Mannering. "The last time, he was sitting in my car—as in Simon's. He had a blackjack and was ready for trouble, but things didn't go well for him, and I delivered him to Ephraim Scoby Esquire." His glance at the girl was swift and piercing, but her face looked blank; or as blank as it ever could, she was full of personality as a balloon should be of helium. "Scoby appears to be his boss. Darling——" He turned to Lorna, hands raised slightly, expression rueful and woeful at the same time. "I'm dreadfully afraid that——"

"You ought to go to see him," Lorna said heavily.

"Yes."

"Well, you can't." Lorna moved back, but not as far as the stool. She didn't smile. She looked severely magnificent. "Toby is your oldest and closest friend. This is his twentieth-wedding anniversary, remember? Only the family and close friends will be there. You are proposing their health. And," she added with forbidding emphasis, "you're *coming*."

"Let me go and see Ephraim," suggested Susan Pengelly brightly.

"Do you know where Simon is?" Mannering asked.

"At his flat. I made him swear that he would stay there until I arrived. He knows I'm here. He admitted that he was afraid that if he came too he would start a fight. The truth is, he wouldn't believe you; that man Ringall was far too persuasive. I'm not really sure that *I* believe you."

Mannering stood eyeing her.

Lorna said: "It's just on seven, John," in a commanding voice.

Mannering said: "Sorry. Yes. Do you know what I would do if I were you, Miss Pengelly?"

"No. What?"

"In spite of the threat to Joy Lessing," Mannering said quietly, "I would go to the police. I'd tell them everything. I'd answer all their questions. And I'd go at once."

The girl said, as if taken aback: "So you would! And how would you stop Simon from wringing my neck?"

"I wouldn't tell Simon what I'd done," said Mannering, and then moved swiftly towards the door, beamed at Lorna, said with dancing gaiety: "Sorry, Sue, I must go and get changed. See me tomorrow, or telephone me late tonight."

He went out of the room, and a moment later a door opened and closed with a bang.

"Does he *mean* that?" breathed Susan Pengelly.

"I've never known him frightened of the police yet," said Lorna Mannering; and she smiled, as if she knew that she had never told a greater lie.

. . . . .

Chittering rang up, soon afterwards, and Lorna took his message. Prinny had not been held by Bristow, and was back in his shop.

. . . . .

The Plenders lived in a graceful square, where one could still hear the clip-clop of horses' hooves, and see tall footmen, hear the crack of the whips, see the sheen on the coats of chestnuts or bays, or fine grey horses, or black or piebald; if one's mind would carry that far. By day there was no room to squeeze a perambulator in the square, but by night there was ample room for parking. So Mannering took the Rolls-Bentley.

Half-way to the square he said: "I may have to leave straight after the speech."

"I don't mind what time you leave after it," Lorna said, "but you're staying until you've made it, even if I have to rope you to me."

"Yes, dear," murmured Mannering. "Dinner at seven forty-five, speeches at nine-thirty, over by ten, and I fly."

After that he drove in silence, Lorna snug in a black Persian Lamb coat, the diamond of a tiara sparkling in her black hair. Flunkeys were on duty in the square, for the Plenders had a long ancestry, the house had been in their family from the day its door had first opened two hundred years ago, and on rare occasions they liked to rekindle memory of the spacious days for those who had plenty of this world's goods.

Inside the hall, lit by fifty lamps in a glistening Spanish chandelier, the Plenders looked not a day more than forty. The Mannerings were the last guests to arrive. Lorna was apologetic, Toby Plender's wife told her not to be silly and carried her off to mysterious regions. Toby Plender grinned at Mannering and, as they went to join thirty or forty men and women waiting and drinking in an *ante* room to the dining-room, he said with mild irony:

"I see you have your name in the papers again."

"Blame the papers. Toby—how much will you forgive me for?"

"Nothing."

"I must telephone Bristow. I may have to go and see him. I left it until I had Lorna here, if I'd called from the flat she would have used a frying-pan on me or else refused to come alone. Unless the Devil or Bristow makes it impossible, I'll be back for the toast."

"That's all right, John," Toby Plender said, and wasn't fooling. "Try to get back. I'll calm Lorna down. If you can't make it, the Old Boy will say the nice things for you. Big trouble?"

"For some people," Mannering said.

He went to a telephone in a room where the cackle of voices sounded as if from a long way off, and where he was alone. He did not feel alone. He felt as if he were being crowded by shadows and watched by ghosts. He dialled Scotland Yard and waited, and seemed to feel the weight getting heavier; the weight which fear places upon the human heart. He did not really know why he should be so afraid. He did not know this Joy, except to recall a pretty, animated face and golden hair and a provocative little figure——

"Scotland Yard, can I help you?"

"Superintendent Bristow's office, please."

"I'm sorry, sir, Superintendent Bristow is in AZ Division at the moment."

"Do you know why?"

"Just a moment, sir, I'll put you through to the Chief Inspectors' office."

"Right," said Mannering. "Thanks." He waited. He had to tell Bristow—and he preferred Bristow to any policeman—that these threats had been uttered against Joy Lessing; also that she had disappeared. He could not take risks with the girl's safety, perhaps with her life. He was sure that Bristow would handle it with all the discretion that it demanded, and wished Bristow were in his office.

A man spoke.

"Who'ssat?"

"John Mannering," Mannering said. "I was hoping

to have a word with Bill Bristow. Is he coming back soon?"

"Shouldn't think so," the Inspector said. "He's over at AZ. Murder job. You'd know the poor beggar. Chap named Prinny, Abe Prinny. Did a bit of fencing, although we never caught him with the goods. Head bashed in. Shop turned inside out. Nasty job, we'd had him here for questioning, the devils must 'a been waiting for him in his shop after we let him go. We'd searched and drawn blank. Bristow's flaming mad, so unless it's urgent, I'd keep away from him tonight."

"Oh," said Mannering very heavily. "I see."

13

A VISIT TO EPHRAIM SCOBY

MANNERING knew Bowing's Hotel well. He also knew the porters. He had no difficulty in getting Ephraim Scoby's room number—302—and none in finding his way to the room. It overlooked a square as quiet and as nostalgic as that where Lorna at this moment was discovering that he had betrayed her.

He listened at the door, made sure that he could hear no one speaking inside, and slid a pick-lock into the key-hole.

One man could take a car engine to pieces and put it together again, another could invent explosives, a third could amass fortunes, a fourth grow onions; Mannering could open doors and force locks of all kinds. He had once been an expert *par excellence*. He had, in fact, once been a cracksman extraordinary, to coin a phrase, and in those days he had won much notoriety and not a little fame as the Baron, who always worked strictly *incognito*. He regarded them as the good or the bad old days, according to his mood, and always remembered them when, as now, he turned the lock with hardly a sound.

He pushed the room door open.

There was a little lobby, with pegs for hats, coats and dressing-gown. Opposite the pegs was the bathroom, on Mannering's left. Opposite the passage door, facing Mannering, was the main bedroom door. The bathroom was in darkness, but the bedroom light was on.

That door was ajar.

Mannering pushed it a little wider.

The smooth-faced man, his jowl darker now because of a few extra hours' growth, sat in an easy-chair with the light above his head, and his feet up on the double bed. He had the evening paper in front of him; it rustled slightly. He wore horn-rimmed glasses. Those, his stubble and his jet black hair threw up the sallow tinge of his skin. He was quite a strong-looking character, and a half-smoked cigar was in one corner of his mouth.

"Ephraim," Mannering murmured.

The man started. His hands must have moved fully an inch, and the paper jumped and rustled. He began to turn his head, but checked the movement, showing remarkable control of his nerves. He raised his head slightly, and looked away from the newspaper, but not at Mannering. He was looking into a mirror.

"How is dear Chas?" asked Mannering, and went farther into the room.

Now, Scoby turned to face him, taking off his glasses and blinking while his eyes refocused. In his way, he was handsome.

"If you mean Ringall," he said, quite steadily, "you shouldn't have made an enemy of Ringall."

"Prinny shouldn't have made an enemy of you, either."

"I don't know what you're talking about."

"The judge, the jury, the prison Governor, the death-cell warders and the hangman will enlighten you, little by little and in due course," Mannering said expansively. "I shall give them some of the information, for I have just

A VISIT TO EPHRAIM SCOBY

come from the police. They know about Joy Lessing. They know a lot of things. Don't hurt Joy."

Scoby said: "Have you gone crazy? Who's this Joy?"

"Simon's sister." Mannering moved again. Scoby didn't seem to be frightened, but probably was. He shifted the cigar from one side of his bloodless mouth to the other. His face still had that powdered look. He hitched himself up a little higher in his chair, and his right hand went towards his coat pocket. He was the kind of man who might carry a gun, and would use one whenever he thought that he could avoid being found out, or whenever he thought that he might be legally justified in doing so: as now, by shooting an intruder.

He gave a slow, almost a pleasant smile; gold-tipped teeth glinted.

"Why don't you cut out the dramatics, Mannering? Let me get you a drink, and——"

"No, thanks," said Mannering. He stepped round the man and rested lightly against the dressing-table. "A rat from all angles. I don't know who or what gave you the idea that I have the Fioras. I haven't. You were fooled. Whether you believe that or not, send Joy Lessing back, tonight."

"This Lessing," Scoby said, "he's dangerous. He's a killer when he's tight. But never mind Lessing. I don't know about this Joy, perhaps you'll explain to me later. I wanted a talk with you."

Mannering took out cigarettes.

"I've ten minutes," he said.

"I want the Fioras," Scoby told him, very slowly. "I know you have them, and I want them. I can get them the hard or the easy way. I've a market for them. I can afford to pay you. I can cut you in to the tune of ten thousand pounds. That's money. There isn't another thing I want, Mannering, just those diamonds—and you can call yourself lucky that I offer as much."

"I do not know where the Fioras are."

"Okay, okay, so you'll stall," said Scoby, and dropped the newspaper. His hand wasn't so near his pocket now, apparently he felt sure that he wouldn't be attacked. "I'm in no hurry. But when I've got those diamonds, everything will be fine, no one will get hurt. Not even you, or any girl friends. Not even Simon Lessing."

Mannering said: "Why did you try to drown Francesca?"

"Say that again."

"What did you do to Bernard Lisle?"

Scoby didn't like this. It showed in the way his eyes narrowed, and the way his hands tightened. Next moment he was normal again, except for one thing. He smiled. To smile more easily, he took the cigar from his lips.

"And they told me you were good," he sneered.

Mannering lit a cigarette. He leaned against the dressing-table with his ankles crossed, studying the man as a bacteriologist would study a smear on a slide. He wondered whether Scoby was known to Scotland Yard, and wondered what gave him his confidence.

"Ephraim," Mannering said, "you're taking a lot of chances with me. Didn't anyone tell you that I work with the police? They'll act on my advice more often than not. And this time I could advise——"

"Advise nothing," Scoby said. He put the cigar back into his mouth. "I'm on to you, Mannering. You've got a good game, but it doesn't always pay off. It won't this time. You can't put the police on to me, and if you could they couldn't touch me. No, sir. I've got alibis. They're good, and they can't be broken. And if you try breaking them or breaking me, I tell the police how I know you have the Fioras. If I don't get them, you won't keep them. Now we ought to understand each other."

He stood up. He was solid, if inclined to run to fat, and his waistcoat was rucked up from sitting, so that his white shirt showed between his waistcoat and trousers. He pulled the waistcoat down. He was so calm and deliberate that he fascinated Mannering.

Then he said with venomous swiftness: "Now get out! Get those diamonds and bring them back here. If you don't want trouble, do just that. Don't try talking me down. You got a wife, you've got friends, there's this Joy, there's Lisle's kid. They can all get hurt, and you can get hurt, too. Bring it all, Mannering. You lord it over the little fences while they take the risks, but do you know what I can do? I can kick everything you've built your phoney reputation on from under you. And I will. Quinns and all the rest. So get out, and fetch me the Fioras. Don't tell the police, don't tell anyone. Get going."

He stopped.

The room was very quiet.

Mannering stood up, slowly. He began to smile, as if genuinely amused. For the first time, Scoby seemed to be puzzled, a little unsure of himself. He moved back to the bed, as if expecting Mannering to strike him. Mannering didn't, but the smile turned into a chuckle, as if he couldn't keep it back, and the situation was too funny for words.

"How the gods must be laughing," he said. He bent down and picked up the shiny black shoes from the side of Scoby's chair. He looked at them.

Scoby said: "What——"

"Hand-made, too." He moved with sudden speed, making Scoby jump, but all he did was to pull open the door of the wardrobe. In one of the lower sections, tight in their chromium trees, was another pair of shiny black shoes. Mannering picked them up.

"What the hell are you doing?" Scoby demanded, and his voice had an edge to it. Mannering had broken his confidence.

"Collecting shoes," said Mannering. "Your shoes. Thanks. May I borrow a case? I'll send it back." He picked up a small suit-case, dropped it on the bed, opened it, and turned the contents out on to the bed; there were only odds and ends. He put the shoes in and closed the case. "Thanks, Ephraim."

"You damned fool, give me my shoes back! I haven't any to wear."

"Work some miracles," Mannering said, "or do it your usual way—steal some, Ephraim." He moved towards the passage door, backing away because he wasn't quite sure how Scoby would react; he still thought it possible that Scoby carried a gun.

But the danger didn't come from Scoby.

The door communicating with the next room opened and Charlie Ringall slid in. He carried the cosh. He had it raised as high as his shoulder, and crouched, as if he were going to jump. He wouldn't be easy to handle in that first assault. The odds were two to one, and Ringall had old scores to settle.

Mannering, the small case in one hand, just flung it upwards at him. As the young brute dodged, Mannering went forward and snatched at the wrist holding the cosh. One twist and Ringall winced as if in agony. The cosh fell.

Scoby stood with his right hand at his coat pocket.

"I don't know whether you carry a gun or not," Mannering said, retrieving the suit-case, "and I'm not interested, Ephraim. I do know that the police found footprints on the Festival Hall Terrace last night. Yours, I think. These shoes will show. They'll go to the police with your name tag on them unless Joy Lessing returns to her flat, tonight." He was at the passage door, putting out a hand behind him, to turn the handle. "Then we'll talk about other things. Joy first."

He opened the door, with his back to it. The strain on his wrist was unexpectedly sharp. He backed into the passage suit-case in hand—but didn't get far. He felt a hand at the back of his neck, the grip of powerful fingers, remorseless pressure which thrust him forward. He tried to turn, but a man kicked the back of his knees savagely. He crumpled up, unable to help himself. He felt himself pushed, fell into the little lobby, and then heard Charlie Ringall rasp:

"Lemme get at 'im!"

He knew it was going to hurt like the devil. He covered up as best he could, but the cosh smashed on to the top of his head, then on the back, then on his jaw. He just had to take it.

He thought of a dead jewel-merchant; and Prinny with a battered head.

He thought of Toby Plender and the dinner and his speech.

He thought of Lorna.

Then all he could think about was the pain at his head and hands and shoulders beneath that savage rain of blows.

14

A DETECTIVE GIVES A WARNING

The battering ceased, and the relief was unbelievable. Mannering was conscious if dazed, breathing even if he caught his breath each time because pain stabbed through his chest. The respite continued. He heard voices, but did not understand the words. Then he did understand; two men were speaking in French.

"Go and see that he doesn't do anything silly."

"Are you sure you will be all right here?"

"Oh, yes, we won't have more trouble."

Mannering had been the victim of this kind of assault before; and after he had handed it out, there was a certain rough justice in being on the receiving end. The unfortunate thing was that Chas Ringall had received so much that day that he had hardly been responsible for his actions; he'd gone berserk.

Doors closed; odd draughts cooled Mannering's hot forehead. Stockinged feet appeared before his eyes, and the end of a pair of trousered legs. A match scraped. Liquid went *gug-gug-gug* in a glass, and reminded him of Chas after being hit by his own cosh. How often, wondered Mannering, had he gone *gug-gug-gug* in the past five minutes.

French.

Au revoir, Ephraim Scoby had said on the telephone. The Marquis de Cironde et Bles, whose chateau had been a show-piece of the Chateau country of the Loire until it had been destroyed by fire a few years ago, had been the owner of the Fiora collection before the now murdered dealer had bought them. Odd that he could recall that and remember all the details so clearly, even remember having been escorted over the chateau some years before, and regaled with stories of the infidelity of kings.

The stockinged feet drew nearer. A foot moved and touched him on the shoulder, and pain shimmered through his head.

"Come on, get up," said Scoby.

Mannering began to obey. He felt much worse than he had realised. Lying still had fooled him. The pains were still in his head, especially behind his eyes and at the nape of his neck, his shoulders and his left arm. His legs were all right, and he was able to use them as if they belonged to him. At last he sat up, with his back against the bed. To the best of his ability he sat still. It was the room that went round and round; stockinged feet, shiny shoes, the claw feet of wardrobe and chairs, water-pipes, a newspaper; all these were now in a deep chasm yawning beneath him now as far away as the stars.

"Come on," Scoby said. "Get up." He stood in front of Mannering and put his hands on Mannering's waist, a little high. "*Up!*"

Mannering felt as if all the blood in his body was rushing out through his head. He staggered. He felt himself drop into a chair, springs groaned and bounced. Existence was nothing but pain.

Something cold splashed into his face, and shocked him; came again, and was almost welcome. Then a telephone went ting, and Scoby spoke in English: something about some coffee. Then Scoby held a glass to his lips, and Mannering sipped some water.

He felt better; not well, but better. He began to feel in his pockets.

"What are you looking for?" Scoby asked. "Cigarettes?"

A DETECTIVE GIVES A WARNING 103

He thrust a case in front of Mannering. "Take one and get a grip on yourself, Mannering."

Mannering took a cigarette, and remembered Bristow telling him about a stub of a Virginia One. His mind was working, some cause for congratulation. He accepted a light, and the flaring match was strong enough to hurt his eyes. He didn't wince.

The smoke was good; soothing.

"Thanks."

"You've got a lot more to thank me for than that," said Scoby. "If I'd let him do what he wanted, you wouldn't have a face, you'd just have an interesting experiment for a plastic surgeon. Now you know what you're up against."

Mannering didn't speak.

"Listen to me," said Scoby flatly. He sat on the side of his bed; Mannering was in the armchair. "When I say a thing I mean it. I want the Fioras. I know you've got them. I don't want a lot of trouble, though. You can still get your sidekick of ten thousand pounds, if you cough up quickly. But don't make me work for them, or you'll be in a lot of soup you didn't expect, and other people will get hurt. You know what I mean by hurt? A fragile little doll like Joy Lessing would really get hurt, wouldn't she?"

Mannering managed to mutter: "Don't you touch——"

Scoby grinned. "Soft-hearted, aren't you? You do what you're told and she'll be all right, everyone will be all right. Don't worry. Just don't try bluffing me any more. You daren't tell Bristow anything, because of what I can tell him about you and the Fioras." A faint note of uneasiness crept into the flat, unattractive voice. "And you couldn't do me any harm, whatever you said to Bristow. You got beaten up, sure, but only because you started throwing your weight about. Who's to say I didn't find you in the room, snooping around?"

Mannering didn't speak.

"What's that crap about shoes?" asked Scoby. "Come on, what's it about?"

Mannering gulped. "I wanted—to scare you."

Scoby grinned with satisfaction. It was what he wanted to believe, and he believed it. Then there came a knock at the outer door. He went to open it, took a tray from the floor waiter, and came back.

He poured out coffee.

"I hope you know when you're beaten," he said, "because a lot of worse things can happen, Mannering." He stirred in plenty of sugar, and brought a cup across. "Drink this. I'm not a bad guy, I don't want to hurt anyone, but I've got things to do, see?"

Mannering sipped, and winced when the hot coffee stung a cut lip. He put a cigarette up to his lip, and when he looked at it there was a smear of fresh blood. He groped for a handkerchief.

"You can go into the bathroom and tidy up in a minute," said Scoby, "but drink that coffee first."

Mannering drank it; slowly. He felt much better. He wasn't quite sure what was the best thing to do—bluff and bluster, or leave here with his tail between his legs. If he were too humbled, it would seem suspicious to Scoby later, even if it didn't now. He took out his own cigarettes, lit one from the stub of Scoby's, then squashed Scoby's out in an ashtray.

"You'll never get away with it," he said.

Scoby's manner changed on the instant. He raised a clenched fist, and glowered.

"You get to hell out of here and get those diamonds! I'll send word where you're to take them. Don't try any tricks, don't think you can fool me. I *know*, see?"

Mannering gulped. "O-Okay."

Scoby grinned again. "Now go and clean up," he said. "Just remember that there'll be cleaning up to do on others if you don't jump to it."

Mannering said heavily: "All right, Scoby, but get this straight. If any harm comes to Joy Lessing, I tell the police about you and Ringall, and I don't give a damn for the consequences."

A moment's disquiet touched Scoby's eyes.

A DETECTIVE GIVES A WARNING

"I'll give the orders," he said. "Quit."

Mannering went out.

. . . . . .

From a telephone booth in the foyer, he called Larraby at his lodgings and asked him to come and watch Scoby, and gave him all the information he could. Larraby promised to come at once.

The cold night air stung his face, especially his bruised lips. The hotel commissionaire looked at him oddly as he said good night, and Mannering couldn't smile a response, his lips were too swollen and painful. He had brought his car, but didn't feel like driving, so he beckoned to a taxi. The commissionaire shrilled a supporting whistle which cut Mannering's head in two.

"Thanks."

"Pleasure, Mr. Mannering. Where to, sir?"

"Whitechapel High Street."

"Yes, sir. Whitechapel High Street," repeated the commissionaire to the taxi-driver. When the taxi had gone, he rubbed the back of his neck, mildly puzzled. Mannering was dressed for the West End and was going to the East. He had come in smiling and startlingly handsome, and was going out looking as if he had toothache.

Mannering smoked a cigarette.

No one followed him.

The City was deserted, it wasn't until he reached Aldgate that light and life appeared again, offering evidence that London was not, after all, a city only of the dead or the dying. He was not greatly interested.

He paid off the taxi at the corner of the narrow road where Prinny's shop was. A crowd was outside the shop, police cars were there, and Bristow's car was there. Two uniformed policemen were trying, with no success at all, to move the crowd along.

One looked at Mannering.

"Sorry, sir, but——"

"My name is Mannering. Ask Mr. Bristow to spare me a few minutes, will you?"

"Mr. Man—oh, *Man*nering. It'll be all right for you to go in, sir."

"Thanks," said Mannering. "They moved the body yet?"

"No, sir, still taking photographs."

"Oh. Thanks."

Mannering went into the shop, which was so brightly lit by arc lights brought by the police that it might have been an amusement arcade in Brighton on a night in August. It was almost as crowded, too. Half a dozen policemen and a police-surgeon were clustered at the far end. Bristow was talking to a block of a plain-clothes sergeant named Ross. One man, with a camera on a tripod and a flash-lamp in his hand, was in the doorway of the room at the back of the shop.

The lamp flashed.

"That'll do," Bristow said to him. "Got the measurements and everything by now, haven't you? We'd better get him away."

"Right, sir."

"The ambulance will be here in a few minutes," Ross said.

"Good." Bristow lit a cigarette. His hand was steady, but he looked very tired. The patches beneath his eyes were almost black, and he showed every month of his fifty-five years. His eyes glistened like those of a man who hadn't had enough sleep. "Okay, get the report——"

"Hallo, Bill," Mannering said.

Bristow jerked his head up. Everyone else looked at Mannering, too, but Bristow was the only one who mattered. He didn't speak at first. He widened his eyes when he saw Mannering's face and the little brown spots on his otherwise snow-white shirt.

"What do you want?" he demanded brusquely.

"A word with you."

"Can't you see I'm busy?"

"This matters."

Bristow took his cigarette from his lips and smoothed his moustache with his forefinger, itself a dark brown from nicotine.

A DETECTIVE GIVES A WARNING 107

"All right, what is it?"

"In private, Bill."

Bristow opened his mouth, and judging from his expression he was going to say "no". Something had happened to change his attitude since their earlier meeting, and Mannering felt reasonably sure what it was. He didn't blame Bristow. He didn't blame anyone, except Ephraim Scoby, Chas Ringall and any unknown gentleman who worked with them. He was as much on edge and nervous as he was ever likely to be.

Bristow changed his mind.

"All right," he conceded, "better come to the back."

He led the way into the small room beyond, which was living-room, stock-room and kitchen combined. Abe Prinny had lived here. Prinny's wife was probably with neighbours, or else the police were taking care of her. Prinny's body lay near the window. A policeman was drawing a sheet over his head, but Mannering caught a glimpse of the blood and the unrecognisable forehead. He shivered, as if ice had been dropped down his back.

Bristow led the way to an even smaller room, beyond; a scullery. The light was on. Water tipped from a tap and splashed into a porcelain sink. There was a smell of cooking; frying, mostly. Wooden shelves fixed to the walls by brackets were weighed down with saucepans, jars filled with a great variety of household needs, crockery, cake-tins, meat-dishes; there was no larder and no store cupboard, so everything was on show.

"I don't know what you want," Bristow said, "but before you start pulling any fast ones, I've got something to say to you. Don't play fast and loose. I'm told you're holding the Fioras, and that someone's after your blood for them. I don't need telling that you've had a beating-up, and if you're poking your nose into this job from the wrong side, you deserve it. Understand?"

Mannering said: "Judge, jury, witnesses and prosecuting counsel, all in one."

"I'm not being funny."

"No," said Mannering, shaking his head slowly. "No, Bill you certainly are not. Who told you this?"

"That doesn't matter a damn. What matters is that it squares up with other things. You were here at Prinny's this morning. Larraby's on his rounds, too."

"As requested," Mannering said. "By the police. By some astounding coincidence, I was looking for the Fioras."

"Which you're sitting on. Oh, I don't doubt that you're doing so for some high-flown motive, such as helping Francesca Lisle, but——"

"Whoever sold you the idea certainly sold it to you," Mannering said. "Green-eyed Susan Pengelly?"

"Never mind."

"Or Simon Lessing? Did anyone tell you that Lessing's sister, a nice little thing named Joy, has been kidnapped. In broad daylight from central London in this year of grace, nineteen hundred and——"

Obviously Bristow knew.

Mannering went on: "Handle it cautiously, please. No matter what you feel about me, be very careful with Joy Lessing. Don't go blundering, as you did with Prinny. Why come to Prinny?"

"I'd had a squeal, saying he had Francesca Lisle's jewelled cross. So——"

"First, ask a benighted stooge like me to look for the jewels, then get a squeal, then put on all steam to show the stooge what a nincompoop he is. I don't think I'm happy about our long, sweet friendship, Bill, it's going on the rocks." Mannering gave that thrust time to register, and then added: "Now, some facts, if your mind can be prised open to accept them. A—I have no Fioras and do not know where the Fioras are. B—You are not alone in thinking I have them, and the story has been spread most convincingly. C—Francesca Lisle was almost killed, the motive wasn't simply theft, and if you let her loose tomorrow without a watchdog you'll be guilty of criminal negligence. D—I tried to borrow a pair of shoes tonight, but failed. I did get some cotton-wool and a cigarette-end which might be the same as those found on the Terrace last night. That's if you'll be gracious enough to check." He paused again, then added: "Last item: Good night."

He turned on his heel and went out.

* * * *

He had to help Joy, this girl he hardly knew.

It was nearly ten o'clock when he was sitting in a taxi and heading for the West End. It was too late to go to the Plenders, and if he appeared with his present facial decorations, he would cause a sensation. If he did what he felt like doing, he would go to the flat and wait for Lorna, consoling himself with brandy, which Lorna would promptly turn into a cup of tea.

Or he could go and see Simon Lessing.

Or visit Susan Pengelly, who had taken him at his word.

Would Bristow be persuaded by the girl that he had the Fioras? The trouble was his past; the ghostly past. When someone whispered this kind of *canard* into Bristow's ear, it induced a kind of mental ectoplasm. Bristow remembered a legendary figure known as the Baron. Bristow had suffered at the hands of the legend and the figure. Bristow knew, but could never produce evidence that Mannering had then been the Baron. Only a policeman of exceptional strength of mind and unswerving sense of purpose could ever have made himself work with such a character, even if reformed. Bristow could. But the breath of suspicion immediately became gale when it blew about Mannering.

It was a pity. There was no doubt that Simon Lessing had now virtually lost faith; Bristow was full of genuine suspicion and there was only Francesca left to serve. Francesca and other ghosts; of the murdered dealer who had lost the Fioras, and now of Prinny. There was also the wispy, vaguely-remembered charm of a Joy Lessing.

It was not nice at all to think of her in the hands of a youth like Chas Ringall.

Lorna wouldn't be home yet.

Mannering had looked up Susan Pengelly's address.

He told his taxi to take him to Henrietta Street, Covent

Garden, paid the man off, and stood at the corner. No one was in sight. A smell of fruit and vegetables, not all gone rotten, was wafted gently from the market. The street cleaners had done a good job, there was not even a cabbage leaf to slip on.

He reached Susan Pengelly's flat. It was in darkness. He produced a skeleton key, gave himself another demonstration of his skill, and went in.

15

THE CURIOSITY OF A RED-HEAD

MANNERing used a pencil torch with a beam-diffusion gadget so that he had just enough light to see without throwing any beyond the window. He went to the window. It was a fine night, a fact which he hadn't noticed outside; the stars were very bright, and the moon seemed near enough for a day-trip. He felt the curtains; they were thick and heavy. He pulled them, and they ran easily on oiled runners. That done, he felt that he dared put on the light.

He went back to the door, and switched it on.

He stood for a moment, getting used to it and looking round. Easel and desk in the corner, with the canvases, were familiar sights. The portraits on the walls were striking; all savage portrayals, just what one would expect from a woman with a big, loose mouth like Sue's. He had an impression, looking at the portraits and at the dazzling screen, that the girl was a primitive; this was the kind of art that an undisciplined genius might reveal—the genius being for likeness and colour.

There wasn't much to search.

Mannering went to the desk first; it wasn't locked. He opened it, and found a startling self-portrait of Sue Pengelly; all the savagery she showed in her subjects showed in this; she hadn't spared herself, and saw herself as others saw her.

She loved Simon Lessing.

She declared it and boasted of it. She had talked about him making a fool of himself about Francesca. Did she hate Francesca? Someone had tried to murder Francesca, and there was no known motive. Not theft only, as far as Mannering knew. They could have stolen her cross and any other jewels she had, without trying to kill her.

Did Sue want her dead?

What other motive could there be?

Francesca might have recognised a thief, and so doomed herself to die. Imagine a man like Ephraim Scoby, and it was easy to believe that such a motive would be enough.

Mannering put the self-portrait aside. There was nothing else in the drawer. He closed it. There was two shallow drawers on one side of the kneehole, a deeper on the other. He opened them all, and the thing he hoped to find was in the last: a magnificent record of the curiosity of red-headed Susan about Francesca Lisle and her father.

There was no given explanation of that curiosity, just a remarkable record. Several reports from a well-known private inquiry agency had been summarised by one person: obviously by Susan Pengelly. Using the inquiry agent, she had probed deeply into the lives of Lisle and Francesca. Here was a record of where they went together, what they did together; here was a note of the sudden accession to fortune, the story of shares which had suddenly increased a hundred-fold in value. Against this entry were three question marks and two interrogation marks, in red pencil. A kind of sneering: *"Oh, yeah?"* Other entries had similar marked commentaries. A graphic story unfolded: that Bernard Lisle had no ordinary business, used an office for appearance's sake, and called himself a Commission Agent. He often went to France——

France!

Remember *au revoir*; and a brief conversation in excellent French.

There were the dates of all Lisle's journeys, too, there were entries which showed that he occasionally went to the East End of London—usually immediately following a visit to France—and called upon jewel-merchants in a small way of business.

Susan's red-pencilled comment was: "*Fences?*"

Prinny wasn't named, but Mannering knew some of the men who were, and Susan's guess was right.

Before Mannering finished the study, it was obvious why Susan had gone to all this trouble; and she gave it away after all, with a succinct remark after one of Lisle's visits to an East End fence. "*How would S. like this?*" S. for Simon. She was searching for anything which would discredit Bernard Lisle and might discredit Francesca. She had almost given up trying to find evidence against Francesca herself, because a last bitter remark was: "*Virginal and too good to be true.*" That would describe Francesca to any cynic.

Mannering put the book away.

He spent five more minutes looking round, but found nothing to suggest that Susan Pengelly knew Scoby, the boy Chas Ringall or anyone else in the affair. But there was an interesting little indication of her love for Simon Lessing. Tucked into a drawer of a small bedside table was a crayon sketch; a smiling Simon to a T. It was easy to believe that she had put it away quickly when Simon had come to see her that afternoon.

A witch, in love.

What wouldn't a witch do to win her love?

Mannering went to the door, listened, heard nothing but, with memory of what had happened at Bowing's so vivid in his mind, opened it with great care. No one was on the landing. He walked down, keeping close to the wall to avoid as much creaking as he could. No one was in the tiny hall. He slipped out into the street.

A taxi turned the end of the road, and thirty seconds later it pulled up outside Susan Pengelly's door.

Mannering went back to the front door, but there was no ground for hoping for sensation. Susan had come home, alone. She paid off the taxi, and as it moved away her tiny feet clattered on the uncarpeted stairs up to her room.

. . . . . .

It was half-past ten.

Lorna wouldn't be home yet, Mannering knew.

The police would probably be watching Bernard Lisle's office; they would certainly have searched it by now. They might have missed something though. The beating-up at the hotel, followed by Bristow's change of attitude, had put a kind of iron into Mannering's soul; it would stay for to-night at least. He'd been hurt, and he wanted results quickly, so that he could hurt back. Above all, it would be good to make a fool of Bristow, even just a little fool.

He went to Chancery Lane.

Bernard Lisle's office was in one of the old buildings near the Holborn End. It housed a detective agency as well as a small press and photograph agency, so the street doors were open all night. Mannering kept a close watch on the doorways and the buildings opposite for fully ten minutes, before coming to the conclusion that if the police were watching, they were doing so from a window or from somewhere inside Lisle's building.

Mannering pulled on thin rubber gloves, turned up the collar of his coat and tugged down the brim of his hat, walked briskly along, and turned into the building. He went just to the top of the first flight of stairs. A door was close by, and the room beyond that in darkness. He proved that practice was speeding up his time on forcing locks; but this was an old-fashioned lock and no challenege. He slipped inside, leaving the door ajar, and watched the staircase.

He saw and heard nothing.

Did Bristow think that it was a waste of time looking after Lisle's office? Did he think it was the last place that Lisle would go to? Or where enemies of Lisle would visit? Or was it just that the forces of the law were stretched so thin that Bristow couldn't spare a man.

Mannering came out of the office which had given him

shelter, went downstairs and studied the list of names. Bernard Lisle, Commission Agent, was on the third floor. Refusing to be hurried, Mannering made quite sure that he wasn't followed before going up.

Lisle's office was at the end of a long, narrow passage, and bare boards made it impossible to move silently; but no offices on this floor appeared to be occupied by night.

Lisle's office was in darkness.

Mannering flicked out his key, slid it into the lock, manipulated with careless dexterity—and had no results at all.

This door really had a lock that did its job.

He began to smile, almost pleased by this. A job could be too easy, making one careless. He shone his torch, and without the diffused focus it shone very brightly on a small key-hole set in a modern brass lock. This would defeat all first- and second-class students of illegal locksmithing. He studied it for several seconds, then took a flat knife with many blades from his hip pocket.

At moments like these the ghost of the Baron became a benevolent ghost. As one man might be an ordinary and commonplace person nine times out of ten and turn into a genius or a magnificent fly-half or a pilot of breathtaking courage on the tenth time, so Mannering was subject to a kind of metamorphosis. It was John Mannering who opened a door with a key or a skeleton key; it was the Baron who needed a craftsman's tools.

A thief, working by night and in silent darkness, needed a sense of alertness which was far greater than that of an ordinary man. He had to listen for faint and distant sounds; to judge one from another; to acquire a sixth sense telling of danger—as an expert motorist might when on the road. It was above all things a highly specialised craft, and once Mannering had been extremely proud of his skill in it.

Now he simply found it useful.

The door was ready to open in five minutes. He did not open it at first, but paused to listen. His breath was coming swiftly, and his heart pounded.

All seemed well.

He opened the door an inch, left it like that, and listened. Allow Bristow a mede of cunning. Bristow might have decided that the safest thing to do was watch Lisle's office from the inside, so that anyone who did break in would walk right into a policeman's parlour.

On this deathly silence, even bated breathing made an audible sound.

He opened the door wider, slipped inside, and shone his torch. He did not expect to see anyone, it was a precaution which came almost mechanically. He expected a small office, and it was so small that the desk was within six feet of the door.

Sitting at the desk was a man.

Well, he had been a man.

16

A WELCOME HOME FOR MANNERING

MANNERING held on to the torch. The thin, bright beam quivered for a moment, then became steady again. It shone on the pulpy mess that had been a face.

It wasn't that anyone had gone for the face, as far as he could see in that first horrific moment; the whole head had been crushed.

Mannering put out the torch.

He stood there for some seconds, then made himself stand upright. That was the first time he realised that he had been leaning against the door, but now he recollected hearing it click to. He groped for the light switch. He looked towards a corner when he switched the light on.

Then he looked at the dead man. The unwonted pull of nausea tugged at his stomach again.

He couldn't afford to be squeamish.

He had come for some evidence that would help him to find out what Bernard Lisle did for a living, and to find out where the man was. He had been prepared to spend half an hour here. Nothing had really changed, he still had the opportunity to search.

Could he force himself to stay?

He took a step forward.

He heard a sound which came from some way off, and yet found its way through the big office building's draughty passages and bare walls. It was the squeal of brakes; so someone near by was in a hurry. The police were often in a hurry. He was perpetually alert for the police when the mantle of the Baron lay upon him.

He heard an unmistakable footstep—of men hurrying.

He opened the door and stepped into the passage; there, the sound was louder. So was the thudding of his heart. He closed the door with a snap, but the thumping of footsteps on the staircase probably muffled it. He went along the passage, swift as a man fleeing from disaster, past the head of the stairs and towards another office. A bright light came on down below. Strange, shadowy shapes were thrown on the wall as men came racing up, but they had not yet reached the landing below.

Mannering used his skeleton-key like a magician's wand, and felt almost choked, in case this lock was a good one, too. It was no more than a modest test for pupils of Lesson One. He opened the door and slipped inside, closed the door, and saw light and then more shadows against the frosted-glass panel.

Someone said: "Careful!"

Another man said: "That's not going to be easy."

They were looking at the lock of the office door. Other men came up, in less of a hurry. Mannering dared to open his door a fraction. The first big, grey back he saw was unmistakably Bristow's.

"All right, get it down," Bristow said. "Make sure there

are no prints on the outside. If this is a fool's errand——"

Another man, Sergeant Ross, spoke quickly.

"Can't see why anyone should tip us off that Lisle was dead in his office, if he wasn't. It's the kind of thing Mannering might do, if he were looking around. Sure it wasn't Mannering?"

"Yes," grunted Bristow.

Mannering waited for fully five minutes; then the detectives started thrusting at the door with their shoulders. He had recovered from the fright enough to imagine the effect if he should go forward and offer his services. The adult mind could have its silly fancies.

The thudding shook this office badly, and when the door opened, it crashed back.

Mannering was sure what would follow; the light would go on, and be followed by a moment of horrified silence.

He waited.

He heard the click of the switch, then opened his door wide, left it open, and stepped into the passage. Four solid backs were turned towards him, four Scotland Yard men stared upon horror.

Mannering turned away from them, away from the staircase towards another passage, went along it, found what he had prayed for: a secondary staircase. He went stealthily down to the ground floor. He could have gone out the front way, but Bristow would have left at least one man down there.

Mannering saw a door marked: *Cloakroom*. It opened to a cubicle with two hand-basins and a W.C. Above the hand-basins was the window he had hoped to find. He pushed it open, climbed out into a narrow alley, walked along it and found himself on a waste-land of bombed sites, like those at Hart Row.

He made his way across this, until he came to a paved road, and soon he was in Holborn.

Buses were still on the street, but only here and there did he see anyone walking. The pubs were closed, and he needed a drink. Now that the forced excitement of escaping from the police had gone, the effect of the sight of the dead man came back; it was likely to haunt him for a long time to come.

So was another thought.

If there was reason to think the body was Lisle's, and the police had been told it was, then someone would have to identify that body.

He turned and walked towards Oxford Street, thinking of Francesca. That and the battered man was all he could think about. What savagery had done this thing, what purpose was there?

The obvious one: a faked death? A body supposed to be Lisle's, but that of another man?

He was guessing wildly.

He was desperately fearful, for Francesca.

A taxi slowed down. Mannering noticed it, without really knowing what it meant. A cabby called:

"Cab, sir?"

Mannering stopped as if struck, clenched his teeth and swung round.

"*What?*"

"Okay, sir, I didn't mean——"

"Oh, taxi. Yes. Yes, thanks." Mannering had the wit to keep his head down, and got in quickly, calling: "Victoria Station, please." He could get another cab from there. He sat back, lit a cigarette, and tried to throw the memory off; but it wouldn't go.

Victoria was busy with the after-theatre rush hour for suburban trains and nearer-suburban buses. Taxis weren't easy to get. Mannering took a Number 11 bus, which passed the end of Green Street. He was so intent that he went two stops beyond the one he wanted, and had to walk back.

It was not until he was on his own landing that he thought about Lorna, who was almost certainly home now, and—angry?

He hesitated.

He wouldn't be able to reason with her, to jolly her, to woo her into a forgiving mood. Vaguely he knew that she would be justified in being sore, even hurt; but he didn't

A WELCOME HOME FOR MANNERING 119

want one of those occasional estrangements. He wasn't himself. In a moment of self-justification he recalled all that had happened. A long, empty afternoon peopled with unlikely fears. Then in swift succession, Chittering, the sharp lesson to Chas Ringall, Susan Pengelly, the encounter with Scoby, the lesson in reverse. A gap. Prinny. Bristow hostile. The girl artist's flat and then—Lisle?

He felt as if his nerves would start screaming.

He took out his key.

The door opened before he touched the keyhole, and Lorna stood there, still in the lovely gown, white shoulders and arms glowing like marble, eyes clear, direct, accusing——?

He said: "Hallo," and moved towards her, looking into her eyes because he did not feel that he could avoid them. He wasn't going to argue, but he needn't crumple up from the beginning.

He saw the expression change in her eyes.

"John," she said, with a catch in her breath. "Darling!"

Suddenly, he was in the room and the door was closed behind them, and his arms were round her—holding her as if, in fact, she were holding him. Clinging to her. At first, the only thought was of his folly; of course she would not let him down, he need not have built up that strange picture of a vengeful wife. She was everything he could ever want.

Then came the other pictures.

Lorna didn't exactly help him into the bedroom, but soon he was there, collar and bow-tie loosened, sitting back in an armchair.

"Take your shoes off," Lorna said. "I'll get you a drink." He'd even been wrong about that: she didn't say "tea". He kicked off his patent-leather shoes, and they reminded him of Ephraim Scoby's. Yes, he could understand what had happened to him; in seven hours——

Five. A clock was striking twelve.

Lorna came in, with whisky, and if there were soda too, he hardly noticed it. He took it in two gulps, then leaned back, breathing through his open mouth. He was feeling light-hearted already; not burdened with so great a weight. Lorna lit a cigarette and put it to his lips.

"How'd the party go? I was—damned sorry——"

"Toby's father was wonderful," she said. "We couldn't stop laughing."

They couldn't stop laughing.

Suddenly, Mannering began to talk, and he couldn't stop talking. Everything poured out. What had happened, what he had done, what he had thought, what he had seen.

Lorna saw, then, how the hours had been so crowded that the marvel was that he was here now; and that he could talk so coherently.

The spate dried up, at last.

By then, and by dint of artless persuasion and suggestion, he was in bed; mumbling. He took two pills; grumbling. He took a glass of some malty milk drink which he swore was abominable at the first sip, and ended up by enjoying. He slid down into bed. With some surprise, he realised that he was in bed, pyjama-clad, teeth cleaned, and Lorna was still in the black evening-gown. Wonderful figure, and his. Wonderful woman, and his. He ought to have looked forward to coming home.

He was asleep before she was in bed.

. . . . .

By eight o'clock the telephone was ringing. Larraby; to report that Scoby had paid his bill at the hotel and vanished; Larraby's distress was due solely to failing to follow the man.

Chittering; to talk.

Simon Lessing; to demand.

Lorna took all the messages, and refused to wake Mannering; but he was up soon after nine.

. . . . .

Bristow didn't sleep well that night. He did not get home until after half-past one, and his wife, who sometimes hardly realised that his life was amongst crime and criminals, for to her he was normal as the next man, knew that he was really worried. Unlike Mannering, he did not talk; when worried he kept the basic facts to himself. He did drop off, about five o'clock, and the telephone was ringing for him at seven. His wife could not keep the importunate Yard officials from him any later than eight o'clock.

By half-past nine, smudgy-eyed, smoking cigarettes one after the other, he was in his office. There were photographs of Bernard Lisle, mostly obtained from Lisle's flat; and photographs of the dead man. These didn't help at all. There was a list of the contents of the dead man's pockets, and three of them—a knife with a monogram, BL, three visiting-cards with his name and address and a driving-licence in his name, might be taken as evidence of identification. The body measurements were about right; the build was about right; the colouring, too, and the colour of the hair—the little that wasn't blood-stained.

Bristow would have taken the identity almost for granted, but for the damage to the head and face. That kind of sadistic damage was seldom done for its own sake. If the killer had wanted to make sure that he couldn't be finally identified, or that the wrong body should be identified, that was the kind of bashing head and face were likely to receive.

There were body marks.

Slight mole on right hip. Butterfly wing mole on right shoulder, beneath the shoulder-blade—an unusual marking. Appendectomy scar. Slight operation scars behind right knee identified by a police-surgeon as the "tying" operation sometimes used for varicose veins; there was a varicose tendency in both legs. Small brown mole on knuckle of left little finger. Small, red scar, possibly a burn, on left wrist, just above the wrist-bone.

The two last might possibly be remembered by acquaintances, but there was no certainty; and in themselves they would not constitute identification. Bristow faced the simple fact: as far as he knew, only Francesca Lisle could identify her father.

He wouldn't wish any girl, good or bad, to have to do that.

He studied other reports. Mannering's movements, as far as they could be traced, gave him time to have been to Lisle's office. There was no proof. Joy Lessing was still missing. Simon Lessing had been in his flat all night, Susan Pengelly had left him fairly early, and gone straight to her flat. The reports were sketchy, he hadn't enough time to tackle them all thoroughly.

He simply hadn't another witness to identify Francesca Lisle's father; if the corpse were Lisle's. The report from the nursing home was good; she was almost herself again, except for some lingering shock symptoms. She had made it plain that she intended to go home. She must be watched, the danger to her was obviously great.

Bristow finished studying the report, and had a word on the telephone with his Assistant Commissioner. He was told to do what he thought best, which didn't help at all, and went straight to the nursing home. This was in a side street off Great Smith Street, near the Abbey.

Outside the nursing home, squeezed between an Austin Seven of ancient vintage and an American car with sleek, shiny lines, was Mannering's Rolls-Bentley. The sight of it annoyed Bristow. He felt sore because he felt sure that Mannering was playing a double game, the trouble with a man who had once been a thief was that he didn't see things in the way of other men, but had a perverted vision. Bristow wasn't sure, but still thought it likely that Mannering was holding the Fioras—possibly for their new owner, possibly as a bait to catch the original thieves and the murderers.

What was he saying to Francesca?

17

AN ORDEAL
FOR FRANCESCA LISLE

AT that very moment Mannering wasn't saying anything to Francesca. He was sitting and looking at her.

She was up and dressed in a navy-blue dress with many pleats in the skirt. She looked nice, except for her expression, which was—frightened? He thought that fear was there. He didn't know whether it was a hangover from what had happened on the Festival Hall Terrace, or whether there was some other reason for it.

He hadn't told her about the body in the office; at least that wasn't his job.

He felt rested; competent to help.

She said: "Yes, of course I shall go home, Mr. Mannering. It's very good of you to offer to have me at your flat, but I'm sure I shall be all right. If I do feel nervous at night, I—I'll come round to you. But why *should* I feel nervous?" Suddenly she was defiant, and that was the thing which puzzled Mannering more than anything else. "My father is bound to be home very soon."

"It's just possible that he won't," said Mannering quietly.

"I don't believe that anything has happened to him!" There was the defiance again; and perhaps she really meant: "I won't believe." She was pale except for spots of colour; she had been when he had come in.

Simon Lessing and Susan Pengelly had been to see her already this morning. Susan, Mannering knew, had brought an offer of hospitality; she could rig up an extra bed. At least there was no need to dissuade Francesca from that. Simon hadn't said anything about Joy, as far as Mannering knew; but Francesca wasn't telling him everything. Yesterday she had been too dazed to show any emotion, now——

The door opened.

"Excuse me, Mr. Mannering," the sister said, "but Superintendent Bristow is here."

Mannering stood up. "Well, why not?"

"He'd like a word with you privately."

"Oh." Mannering smiled at Francesca, and offered his hand. Hers was very cold. "Don't forget, if there's anything at all I can do, I will."

"I'm sure you will," she said mechanically.

He went out, carrying a mental picture of the girl. Some people would find her exceedingly lovely, but he didn't think much about her looks. Her manner, her thoughts and her fears mattered. Was she thinking that he was involved? Had ardent, impetuous Simon told her of the *canard*? Or had Susan told her, with sweet malevolence, that she was sure that Mannering had those jewels, and was her father's enemy.

He felt sure she had been told something to upset her.

Bristow was in the sister's office; alone, smoking, rubbing his right eye. He stood by the window overlooking the street and, if he turned his head, he could see a stretch of the River Thames. It was sunlit that morning, for the day was mild and bright. Outside, people were walking with a spring in their step.

The sister closed the door on them.

"Hallo, Bill," said Mannering. He looked bruised but much better; the full night's sleep and Lorna's ministrations had served him well. He could even think clearly. "Bad night?"

"I had a hell of a night," Bristow growled. "What have you been saying to that girl?"

"Offering to put her up at the flat."

"Very considerate, aren't you? Anxious to be pally."

"Helpful."

"Why?"

"Bill," said Mannering, keeping his hands in his pockets; they fidgeted almost of their own accord, as if they would like to tackle Bristow, "I know that the Yard's stretched pretty thin. None of you has time to do all you want to, and you haven't enough men to go round. But you won't get anywhere if you don't catch up on sleep."

Bristow glowered: "We'd be better off if we didn't have to waste so much time on——" He didn't finish, gulped, stubbed out a cigarette and—without realising it, Mannering felt sure, took another from a packet of twenty Players. "Did you telephone us about that body at Lisle's office?"

The news wasn't in the newspaper.

Mannering looked shocked; he didn't overdo it, because Bristow would be very alive to excess. He waited for a moment, and then said quietly:

"Are you serious?"

"You know damned well I am!"

Mannering said slowly: "Was it Lisle?"

"Isn't that what you've been talking to the girl about?"

"Bill," said Mannering heavily, "I didn't know about it. If I had——" He paused, moved, lit a match and held it out. Bristow took the light with a grunt. "I don't get it. A body—you didn't say Lisle. Was it Lisle?"

Bristow said: "I don't know. I think so."

"Why can't you be sure?"

"Someone meant it to be doubtful," Bristow said. "It wasn't a nice sight."

Mannering just said: "Oh."

"Know anyone else who knew Lisle intimately?" Bristow demanded.

Mannering saw the implications of that, and didn't like them.

"No," he said slowly. "Only Francesca."

"Hell of a job," muttered Bristow, "but I suppose I'd better get it over. The doctor and the sister seem to think she can stand it. Had any more trouble?"

"No."

"Seen Lessing?"

"No."

"His sister's still missing," Bristow growled. "I've put a call out for her." He stubbed out the cigarette. "And don't forget what I told you, if you have those Fioras, you're asking for trouble, and I'll make sure that you get it."

Mannering didn't speak.

Bristow went out.

. . . . .

Bristow reached the street, with Francesca Lisle by his side. She was very pale indeed, now, and walked as if she weren't quite sure where the next step would take her. Bristow's car was at the kerb, not far from Mannering's; Mannering got out of the Rolls-Bentley and came up.

"Going to get it over at once." Bristow was gruff.

"Where?"

"Cannon Row."

"I'll ask Lorna to go over," Mannering said.

"Yes, be a good idea." That was evidence of a thaw.

Francesca didn't seem to hear any of this. She stood listlessly by Bristow's side. Listlessly? Mannering was impressed, as he had been earlier by her obvious fear, but was quite sure that it wasn't fear for herself. Someone or something had frightened her, and Bristow's news had frightened her still more. What had Bristow said? There wasn't much choice for the Yard man or anyone else; he must have told her there was a dead man with a mutilated head and face, and that she was to try to recognise the body.

"This is the car, Miss Lisle," Bristow said, and then swung round on Mannering, who prepared for another outburst. He could not have been wider off the mark. "Come along with us, will you? Be a help to Miss Lisle. We can have a message sent to Lorna from the car radio."

The request was an olive branch in itself, as well as a sign of the resurgence of the human being in Bristow.

"Thanks," said Mannering.

He handed the girl into the car, and climbed in after her. Bristow took the wheel. No one else came. Bristow slid the car into the stream of traffic, and then said in an unfamiliar, gruff voice:

"It'll help us both, Miss Lisle, if you'll try to remember

AN ORDEAL FOR FRANCESCA LISLE 127

any—any distinguishing marks on——" He didn't finish, but swerved sharply past a cyclist who seemed to be quite oblivious of his carelessness. "I mean, birthmarks. Or say a mole, or——"

The girl didn't answer.

Mannering said very quietly: "I've a small mole just behind my right ear." He touched his ear. "And a scar on my right forearm, another—a nasty one—on my left shoulder. That's the kind of thing we mean."

Francesca stared straight out of the window, the tears glistening in her eyes. Bristow cleared his throat, ready to talk again, and Mannering said:

"All right, Bill."

Bristow didn't speak.

Francesca said huskily: "He had—he has a birthmark on his right shoulder, a kind of moth. It looks like a small brown moth, or butterfly. And——"

She couldn't go on for some minutes. They were drawing nearer Scotland Yard and the nearby police-station with its morgue and its terror.

Suddenly, she burst out: "He burned his wrist a little while ago, and he had an operation for—for varico——"

She broke off, trembling violently. She seemed oblivious of the fact that she was gripping Mannering's hand.

"He can't be dead," she choked. "He can't be, it must be someone else."

* * *

The morgue was big and gloomy, and struck cold; it had to be kept cold. The windows were all of thick, frosted glass. Over the stone slabs, where bodies lay until the police had finished with them, were electric lights which, when switched on, were very bright. There was no room for sentiment or squeamishness here. Some of the men and women whom Sergeant Worraby fished out of the Thames lay until some sniffing or tearful wife—or son or daughter, father or mother—came to look on a lifeless face and to nod, in real or pretended grief. It was the nearest morgue to Scotland Yard, too, a stone's throw away. The morgue-keeper had been known to boast, if not to gloat, that all the best corpses came here.

Bristow opened the door.

Francesca stepped through, with Mannering close behind her. She put a hand on Mannering's arm, her first gesture of defensiveness. The light was on over a shrouded figure. An attendant stood at the head of the corpse, hands by his sides, demeanour almost one of boredom. There was only the one corpse in the cold room.

A policewoman stood with Francesca.

Bristow said: "As I said in the car, Miss Lisle, I want you to look at the scars. Tell me if you recognise them. You know how important it is, don't you?"

She whispered: "Yes."

"It won't take a minute."

Mannering felt the tightness of the girl's fingers. Obviously every step she took was an ordeal. He thought of the journey from the nursing home, and Bristow's gruff questions, his almost despairing attempt to be matter-of-fact. Bristow hadn't said a word about it, but managed to exchange glances with Mannering, telling Mannering the significance of the scars and marks.

"I'm so frightened," Francesca said, and her words came like little pellets of ice. She clung to Mannering's arm. "It couldn't be——"

Mannering put his other arm round her. Bristow took a corner of the sheet. The girl was trembling violently. It had to be done, and it was damnable; torture and torment together.

The dead man's head was bandaged.

The girl's teeth chattered, and she shook violently. Mannering held her much as he had held Lorna the night before, but to give strength, not to seek it.

The corpse was lying face downwards. The powerful right shoulder showed and, beneath it, the butterfly scar. Bristow shot his questioning look into Francesca's eyes; eyes which were glistening with bitter tears.

"Have you ever seen this before, Miss Lisle?"

She tried to speak, couldn't get the word out, tried again and said, sobbing: "Yes."

Bristow turned the cloth back, took the limp arm quite reverently, held the wrist and raised it to the light. The scar looked very red.

"Have you?" he asked.

"Oh, no, no, no!" cried Francesca. "He can't be dead, he can't be!"

Bristow steeled himself to ask more questions.

18

A MEASURE OF AGREEMENT

MANNERING watched the taxi disappearing. He caught a glimpse of Lorna's face as she glanced round towards him. Then she disappeared along the Embankment. A police car was just behind her, and other police had already gone ahead. In ten minutes Lorna would be in Chelsea, helping Francesca up the stairs to the studio flat. It wasn't a task she relished, but she would do it better than most.

The policewoman was also in the taxi.

Bristow was standing with Mannering, at the foot of the steps of the new building which housed the C.I.D. He still had those smudgy eyes, and looked as if he would break into a yawn at any moment. Mannering turned to look at him.

Bristow said: "We're so short-handed that we're days behind with some jobs, and watching her is going to cost three men. I hope it's worth it." He brooded. "I wish I knew why Lisle was killed, too."

Mannering said: "Why did you turn sour on me?"

Bristow was in the mood to answer.

"Because I didn't like what you did." His tone hardened, for Bristow his manner became almost trucculent. "I still don't. Just because you came in useful——" He broke off.

What he meant was that he had been in a fix, and had known of no one more likely to help than Mannering. There was a moment of complete understanding between the two men, when their defences were right down.

Bristow shrugged and turned away, leading the way towards the main hall.

"You coming up?"

"Yes," Mannering said. He followed the Yard man into the hall, up the two flights of stairs, along a wide passage and into his office. This was long and narrow, with windows broadside on the Embankment, offering a view of Westminster Bridge, the sluggish old river and the squat mass of London County Hall. The sun still shone, the sky was blue and the Thames reflected it, looking calm, peaceful and benevolent—as if it could never take a man or woman or child and hold on with cold indifference until death came.

Francesca had been pulled out of its embrace. Now she was in the tight hold of grief.

There were two desks, but no one was in the office. Bristow flung his hat towards a peg, and missed; it rolled almost to his feet. He kicked it.

"That's how it goes," he said. "Everything I start comes back and hits me in the face. All right, I was wrong to raid Prinny. I suppose what you really mean is that if I hadn't he might not have been dead. That he was killed because——" He broke off.

"Why did you turn sour, Bill?"

Bristow was lighting a cigarette.

"Prinny named you."

"As what?"

"As the man ready to sell the Fioras. Prinny had one of them—the girl's cross, the one her mother was supposed to have had." Bristow rounded his desk, sat down, pulled open a drawer and produced a matchbox. He opened this; cotton-wool inside hid the jewelled cross.

It flashed and flamed.

Mannering exclaimed: "You left that in an unlocked drawer? You must be going crazy!"

Bristow found a grin from a distant place. "They don't burgle Scotland Yard," he said, "and they certainly don't raid it in daylight. After we'd found it, Prinny told me you'd brought it to him, and I knew you'd been to see him. He told me that you wanted him to hold it for you. He said he trusted you, and agreed. He was scared, and I brought him here. He was sitting in that chair for two hours, and we didn't give him a minute's peace. Oh, we didn't third-degree him, but he was fit to drop when we finished. We didn't shake him from his story by so much as a syllable. He was hard to disbelieve. I could imagine that you wanted to make sure that no one found the jewelled cross at Quinns, that you'd be safer without it." Bristow was drawing at his cigarette between the sentences, and that gave the story a curiously disconnected form; he looked steadily at Mannering all the time. "Then this girl Susan Pengelly said her piece. That girl reminds me of someone, and it isn't anyone good."

"Pictures of the knitting matrons of Tyburn," said Mannering, "or the sadistic ladies of Madame Guillotine's Court."

Bristow considered.

"I see what you mean," he conceded. "But if she were a Borgia, Delilah, Circe and Cleopatra rolled into one, and she isn't, I'd have believed her when she said that cosh-boy said you had the Fiora Collection. And I don't believe the slob would have acted the way he did if he hadn't thought so. He certainly wanted Simon Lessing to use his influence on you." That brought a faint smile even to Bristow's cynical lips. "How much he didn't know!"

"Oh, he believed it. He tried the same trick on me."

Bristow looked pointedly at his swollen mouth.

"Young Lessing must be in better condition, he nearly knocked the little swine's head off."

"That's the trouble," Mannering said, "I'm getting spongy and decadent, and you know what it does to the muscles. So you couldn't shake Prinny's story?"

"No."

"He was a funny little chap," Mannering said reflectively. "I liked him, and I think the liking was mutual. He must have been terrified of what would happen to him. Terrified. With reason, too. He was told to name me as the man with the Fioras, and he did just that—for fear of death. I'd forgive him the lies even if he were alive." There was a pause; then abruptly: "Any news of Joy Lessing?"

"No."

"Call out?"

"I told you it was. So you want me to believe that you don't know where the Fioras are."

Mannering looked at the shimmering cross.

"Until just now, my ignorance was even greater than yours."

"What is it you do know? Isn't it time you stopped playing lone wolf, and——?"

"No," Mannering said, very precisely. "I know a little, Bill. I don't know quite how significant. If I pass it on you'll have to take police action. If you take action, I'm afraid that Joy Lessing might die. That's how scared I am of these people. That's why I'm keeping some things to myself. But not the Fioras; I don't know where they are."

Bristow chewed on his teeth.

Traffic noises came in from the sunlit embankment and the sturdy bridge. Big Ben chimed suddenly, the booming note reverberating into and about the room. Twelve noon. So much had happened in so little time.

Da-da-da-da.

Bristow said: "If things go wrong because of what you're holding back, you'll have your own conscience to answer, and I for one wouldn't let it rest. Here's a question you might be able to solve. What makes these people think you have the Fioras?"

"It's the question I'm trying to answer myself."
... *six—seven—eight.*
"It could be important."
Nine.
"Yes, Bill. We have a gap of——" Mannering waited until the last booming stroke faded away; its echo lasted for a long time; after it, his voice sounded very quiet. "Francesca had the jewels with her, there isn't much doubt about that. We know what time she reached the Festival Hall. We know she was found about an hour afterwards. She didn't see her father after he had spoken to her at Waterloo Station—in fact she didn't really see him then. She was attacked, presumably robbed, and then pushed into the river. Why didn't Prinny's killers get the Fiora jewels then? They snatched the cross from her neck. What actually happened to the other stones in that hour?"

Bristow said, as if unwillingly: "I suppose there could be two sets of thieves."

"Wouldn't that be nice? One set believe that I stole the Fioras either (*a*) in person or (*b*) through whoever took them from the girl. Who would tell them that I had the Collection?"

Bristow said stonily: "You're doing the guessing."

"Who would they expect to *know* who had them?"

Bristow's eyes lost their smudgy look, almost for the first time. He stubbed out a cigarette, and forgot to light another. He barked:

"Bernard Lisle!"

"That's right."

"The thieves got them from the girl, Lisle got them back, the thieves tackled him, and to keep in the clear he named you." Bristow couldn't get the words out fast enough.

"It could be that," Mannering conceded, grudgingly.

"And when the gang was sure Lisle hadn't got them and didn't know where they were, they killed him. And telephoned us to report that he was dead? Why do that? It was a man's voice—he just dialled 999 and reported. I happened to be in the Information Room at the time, I'd just got back. So we went there like rockets." Bristow began the inevitable business with cigarettes. "Well, we've worked up a pretty theory."

"Couldn't be prettier," Mannering agreed. "How much attention have you given Simon Lessing and Susan Pengelly?"

"The usual check."

"Found anything?"

"Simon runs a genuine architect's business, he has some money and has a reliable assistant. The girl's a genuine art student, reckoned to be one of the most brilliant at the Slade. Brilliant but uncontrolled. They spent most of the summer and all of their winter vacation in Paris—with two or three others from the school."

"Paris?" echoed Mannering. "Who else went? Francesca?"

"No. Joy Lessing and a couple of other girls. What's on your mind?"

"There's a vague French association already," Mannering said. "I heard two men speaking French in a way which suggests that the people speak it a lot, and where would they do that except in Paris, France? The original owner of the jewels was le Marquis de Cironde et Bles, whose chateau was burned down over his head and who had to sell a lot of heirlooms and family treasures because he'd forgotten the little matter of insurance. Or it had been forgotten for him by a careless secretary. Now these girls study painting in France. Bernard Lisle—have you a photograph of him?"

"Here." Bristow ferreted among the papers on the desk and produced one; a good one. "Handsome beggar," he commented.

"He said the jewelled cross once belonged to Francesca's mother," Mannering said. "Francesca's mother would have been somewhere about the age of forty-seven to fifty, if she'd lived. The cross might have been hers a long time ago. Bill, I think we want to find out how many daughters the Marquis de Cironde et Bles had, and whom they married. That might help us to identify Bernard Lisle. Can you get that from the Sûreté Générale?"

"Yes." Bristow moved to the telephone. "And I'll ask for a photograph, too. You get ideas sometimes. Where are you going now?"

"To see Simon Lessing and Susan Pengelly," Mannering said. "The girl might have met Lisle in Paris, mightn't she? Or met someone who's involved in this from across the Channel."

"You'll probably find the pair at Lessing's flat," Bristow told him. "I'm keeping it watched, and my man reported half an hour ago." He touched a note on his desk.

"Thanks," said Mannering. "Don't lose 'em, Bill."

He used the lift to go downstairs, nodded absently to familiars at the Yard, reached the courtyard and realised that his car was still outside the nursing home. It was only ten minutes' walk away. He decided to walk, for a taxi would probably take longer in the midday traffic. It was so warm that some typists were carrying their suit coats as they walked along the embankment. Mannering kept on the river side, which was emptier. On the gardens just beyond the Houses of Parliament it looked like a summer day. Every seat and every inch of grass was covered with sitting or sprawling bodies, a thousand jaws were chewing on a thousand sandwiches, and a thousand apples were waiting for the onslaught of sharp teeth.

He crossed the road to the side street and his car.

A man, lounging against the wall, moved as he came up, and deliberately blocked his path.

19

MANNERING RECEIVES INSTRUCTIONS

THE man wasn't ill-favoured so much as rugged. He was dressed in a baggy suit of grey tweeds, had a big moustache which looked as if it might come off when pulled hard; and shaggy eyebrows which were probably false, too. He had an easy smile. His movements were lazy but considered, and he gave the impression that he could pack a useful punch.

"Fancy meeting you," he greeted.

Mannering stopped. "You have the advantage of me," he said solemnly.

The other's grin broadened.

"Scoby said you'd see it his way, sooner or later! Now you've seen the kind of thing that happens to people who play fast and loose with us, and we hope it's a lesson you've learnt. You remember there was some talk about those little bits of glass."

Mannering moved, to allow a young girl and an elderly woman to pass.

"Vaguely."

"Better not be vague," the man said. "Scoby wants them tonight. Take them with you to Lessing's flat. Fair exchange—the bits of glass for the bit of fluff." He grinned. "You wouldn't like little Joy to stay with her new friends any longer, so that she could learn a bit more about life, would you?"

The grin was a leer.

"I told Scoby one thing," Mannering said, "don't hurt Joy. Don't hurt her and don't teach her anything." He moved on.

The man took his wrist and held it very tightly, with the pressure of a man who had great physical strength.

"Tonight, Lessing's flat, no police, no pals," he said.

Mannering flicked his wrist. Strength was one thing, judo another, and in days long past it had been necessary for him to fling a sixteen-stone policeman over his shoulder. This man was not sixteen stone. He winced, gasped, felt as if his arm were going to break, and then smacked back against the wall, propelled by what appeared to be no more than a wave of Mannering's hand. Two lads gaped, a nicely-turned out young woman in a veil and pipe-line skirt missed a step.

"I'll be seeing you," Mannering said, and smiled at the man who, remarkably, had ceased to grin.

Mannering didn't quicken his pace. He wasn't followed. He wasn't fooled. Simon Lessing's place was named as a rendezvous, but if he started out for it he would be held up long before he got there. He was beginning to have deep if reluctant admiration for the tactics of Scoby and his men.

His car was still there.

It hadn't been touched, as far as he could judge. He drove straight to Lessing's flat, which was on the second floor, and immediately there was a movement inside.

Simon Lessing didn't open the door; Susan Pengelly did. She looked surprised but not displeased. She opened her loose red mouth and showed those oddly small and widespaced teeth. The light from a window behind Mannering put a glint into the green of her eyes. She wore a smock, gay with colour and much too tight for her. It seemed to extend her massive figure almost to her knees.

"Hallo," she said, "come in." She stood aside. "Si, it's the amateur detective genius."

"Who?" Simon came hurrying from one of the three rooms in sight. He stopped abruptly. "So it's *you*!"

"Honey," Susan said, "the obvious may be left unsaid."

"What do you want, Mannering?" Simon demanded.

The evidence of strain was in his glittering eyes. His hands weren't as steady as they should have been, and as if to point to that, he had cut himself on the right cheek while shaving; there was a hair-thin red line. His lips were set tightly, and moved almost as a puppet's; he wasn't so good-looking this way.

"Well?" he snapped. "Are you going to play ball, or are you——?" Simon broke off. He lunged across the room to a baby grand piano, where several photographs stood in ebony frames. He grabbed one, swung round, and thrust it in front of Mannering's eyes. "See that. That's Joy. That's the girl you're sacrificing for those damnable jewels."

It was an effective move. The photographer had caught Joy Lessing when she was beginning to smile, and when her eyes held a dawning light. Mannering remembered her very well indeed. Lovely. Kissable; crushable; killable.

"Well? You going to stand by and ler *her* suffer?"

"No one should be judged too soon, Mr. Mannering might be an honest man," Susan cooed.

"Honest my foot! He——"

"I know that you must be as worried as a man can be about Joy, but spluttering like a firework display won't help you or Joy," Mannering said mildly. "Do you want to try to find her, or don't you?"

"He comes with the words of a cooing dove and adorns himself in the white petals of deception. Original." Susan started a move into one of the rooms, a nicely-furnished living-room.

"Of course I want to find her," Simon rasped. "And you are the one man who can——"

"No, I'm not," said Mannering. "I haven't the Fioras. But I know now that someone has been fooled into believing that I have. I am instructed to bring them here, tonight. That doesn't give me long to look for them."

Simon ejaculated: "*What?*"

Susan Pengelly slipped off the smock. Underneath, she wore a woollen jumper, obviously self-knitted, with big stitches and several knots where the wool had been badly joined. Incredibly, it fitted loosely.

"Who'd like a drink?" she asked.

"Have they been after you again?" Mannering asked.

Simon didn't answer.

"Yes," said Susan. "Blood-curdling threats uttered in the same kind of disarming voice as yours. It was a man he met in the street. What were the exact words, Si? And when you've time, tell me if you'd like a drink. We can offer," she added, "whisky or gin, gin or whisky, and if you're really particular, a little whisky or gin. No It, but there might be a spot of Noilly Praat."

"The exact words," said Simon speaking as if each breath were being dragged out of him, "were these, as nearly as I can remember them: 'Make sure Mannering plays ball. If he doesn't, your kid sister will be grown up all of a sudden.'" For a moment he was silent, then he blurted out: "The ruddy swine!"

Susan murmured: "Does anyone know which is better for blood-pressure—whisky or gin?"

Simon swung round on her. "Why don't you shut up? You've been making cracks like that all the morning. If you can't keep quiet, get to hell out of here."

Susan Pengelly smiled——

But she wasn't laughing with her eyes at all. His savage manner hurt her. It was impossible to tell whether he knew it, or whether he cared. She didn't turn away, but watched him very closely. Then she spoke.

"What do you really want from us, Mr. Mannering?" She was almost subdued.

"I want to find out how anxious Lessing really is to get his sister back," Mannering said, "and I want to know more about her. There hasn't been time to probe. I know . . ." He told them what Bristow had told him. During the telling, Susan brought him a gin-and-French, and put a different-shaped glass with a different-coloured liquid into Simon's hand. "How well did Joy know the Lisles?"

"The two Lisles?" Simon looked at his drink. "I don't think she knew Bernard Lisle very well. She met him at Francesca's place once or twice, and once in France, I believe. But it was Francesca she was interested in. They are inseparable. What Franky will say——"

"We'll look after Francesca," Mannering said. "Did Francesca often confide in Joy?"

"Suppose you tell us what you're getting at," Simon demanded.

"I want to know why these people kidnapped Joy."

"You know why. So that I could be forced to make you——"

"Simple Simon," Susan gurgled. She did not remain subdued for long. "Even I knew that was phoney. They had Joy and they used her that way, but no one in their senses would ever believe that you, Simon Lessing Esquire, could bring pressure to bear on Mannering. Phoney as they come. I wondered when Mannering would get round to this particular question, even I can see that it may be important. I could venture an opinion, of course, but I'm not sure that it would be welcome."

"May we have it?" Mannering invited.

"Will you protect me?" asked Susan mockingly. "From the wrath to come, I mean. I think that Francesca told Joy something in confidence, and that as a result it wasn't safe for these hoodlums to let Joy run round loose. I think that Francesca's father was a crook. Spelt C-R-O-O-K. That he had these diamonds, and that thief is trying to rob thief. I also think that Francesca knew all this, and——"

"I told you to shut up." Simon rounded on her savagely, eyes glittering. "Now you've gone a damned sight too far. All I ever get from you are foul innuendoes about Francesca and her father. The trouble with you is a mind like a sewer, you can't imagine anyone being decent and straightforward. You—you ought to have been born in the gutter five hundred years ago. Now get out, and don't come back."

She was startled enough to plead.

"Si, don't be——"

"Get out!"

She closed her mouth tightly; there was just a bright red slash beneath her nose. She looked at Simon from narrowed eyes, and the green in them seemed to be shimmering in the light of an emotion which it was hard to understand.

Then she went to the sideboard, poured herself out a finger of neat whisky, drank it as if she were pouring medicine down her throat and, without another look at Simon or at Mannering, went out.

The room door and the outer door closed quietly.

Simon said: "There are times when I hate the sight of her!" He snatched out his pipe and stuck it, empty, between his fine teeth. "Oh, forget her. What do you really want to know?"

"Whether Francesca could have told Joy anything which made Joy dangerous to these people," Mannering said mildly. "Or whether Joy found anything out, unknowingly. Did she hint of anything like that to you?"

"That Lisle was a fence, you mean? No, she didn't. Susan's hinted at it for weeks. But then, anything Susan could do to discredit Francesca was as good as done. Sometimes she scares me."

Mannering murmured: "If she could hate as well as she can love you'd be in hell, my son."

Simon looked startled, but went on quickly: "That's exactly what I mean. The devil of it is that I'm never myself when Sue's around. She makes me feel vicious. I don't know what it is. She's always needling me in some way or other, and since I've—I've become so fond of Francesca, it's got much worse."

"How long is that?"

"Oh, the better part of a year."

Simon began to fill his pipe. He smoked a broad-cut mixture with a sweet smell. He looked as if he had a blinding headache; there was a tell-tale shiny kind of brightness in his eyes. Like Bristow, he hadn't slept much; and to a degree much more than Bristow's he was living on his nerves.

"If you haven't got the jewels, what the devil are we going to do?" he asked abruptly.

Mannering said: "I could pretend that I have. They'll probably be in touch with you again, soon, and may make even uglier threats about Joy. Do you think your nerve can stand up to more strain?"

"Oh, I can take the strain, it's being so helpless that gives me hell."

"When they ask again, give them a message. Say I told you that I'd been ordered to bring the jewels here. Say that I told you their offer was chicken-feed, and that in any case I wouldn't go to them, they'd have to come to me. In other words, let them feel more sure than ever that I have the jewels."

Simon said: "I don't get it."

"Above everything else, they want the diamonds. While they think I have them, there's a hope that they'll string along. And they'll probably go easy on Joy."

Simon said in a strangled voice: "*Probably!*"

"That's right," Mannering said, "and I think they will. If you can fool them."

"I'll fool them," Simon said.

. . . . .

The trouble for the time being was that Mannering knew that he couldn't take the offensive. Now Scoby had just vanished, it was as simple as that.

They were up to all the tricks.

Mannering drove to Quinns, where Larraby reported a blank day of inquiries, too.

"All right, Josh," Mannering said. "Give up the shop for the day, and keep an eye on young Lessing. He'll be approached again, and might be told to go and see Scoby and company. Try to trail Lessing. The police are doing it, but he probably knows that, and it's easy to dodge a man you know about."

"He won't dodge me," Larraby said, as if he had turned from cherub to avenging angel.

. . . . .

Mannering drove to Green Street, with the windows of the car right down. The wind off the river was almost balmy. He turned the corner, and wasn't altogether surprised to see Susan Pengelly standing on the pavement, outside his house. She didn't smile at him, but waited until he got out and approached. Then she said smoothly:

"I'm sorry you were inflicted with Simon's tantrums, but I suppose I had it coming to me. He is evidently not for me." Her eyes brooded. "All the same, I don't want him to get into more trouble. I think Francesca spells trouble for him and for anyone she touches. Including you."

"She might," Mannering said mildly. "I've known the angels be satanic and the ones born bad become angelic." His eyes laughed at her. "Why do you hate Francesca so much, Sue? Because she's taking Simon away from you?"

"No," she said. "Someone was going to do that, anyway, he's not for me. I just don't trust the goody-goods, and I didn't like the effect Francesca had on Joy. Joy worshipped her. She was always with her. I didn't think it was healthy. I think you've got something when you say that Francesca or her father said something in Joy's hearing and put Joy in this spot. Do you think there's any chance of saving her?"

The question came very sharply; almost fearfully.

Mannering said: "I don't know. I simply don't know."

20

NEWS FROM THE SÛRETÉ GÉNÉRALE

LORNA was in Mannering's study, looking through a book of beautifully coloured plates—all pictures of diamonds. She hadn't heard him come in, and looked round with a start when he said:

"You won't find the Fioras in that, sweetheart!"

"Is there a picture here at all?"

"No, only at the office. How's Francesca?"

"She wanted to go home, but the policewoman and I persuaded her to rest here for a bit. I gave her two of those sleeping-tablets I had last month, and she dropped off in ten minutes or so. The policewoman's gone." Lorna was frowning; when frowning, she looked almost sullen. "She was absolutely distracted. Her father complex is so strong that she'll probably get worse and become a psychiatric case. Men like Bernard Lisle ought to be——" She broke off.

"He could have lost a beloved wife, become a psychopathic case himself, and shifted all his love to Francesca."

"That's what did happen, obviously." Lorna could be as illogical as anyone. "It couldn't be more cruel."

"Francesca may be tougher than you think," Mannering said hopefully. "Some women are!" He slid his arm round her waist. "When she comes round, get her to talk about Joy Lessing."

"Will it help?"

"It might," said Mannering. "Three questions of varying importance keep nagging me—and nagging Bristow, who is himself again. Who said I had them and why? What happened between the time Francesca was attacked and when her body was found——"

"Don't say 'her body' like that!"

"You're being too squeamish, my sweet." But Mannering's expression made it clear that he didn't really think so. "And third, why was Joy kidnapped? Sometimes I think that's more important than anything else. Finding Joy might be a good thing for its own sake."

"Do you really think they'll hurt her?"

Mannering simply squeezed her waist again. Then the telephone bell rang, and he went across to it, saying:

"I had a bad time for food yesterday, see what Ethel can manage now, will you?" He lifted the telephone, and Lorna got up but didn't go out of the room, just stood and watched. "Oh yes, put him through." He put the mouthpiece against his chest. "Bristow."

He paused.

NEWS FROM THE SÛRETÉ GÉNÉRALE

There were footsteps outside. "Excuse me, mum——"
"Yes, Ethel, we're ready. Dish up, will you?"
"Yes'm. I didn't want to hurry you, but you know what saddle of mutton is if it's overdone, can't do anything with it. Will Mr. Mannering carve, or shall I?" Ethel hovered in the doorway.

"You carve, will you?"

"Hallo, Bill," said Mannering. "Paris already, that's quick."

Lorna went out, and Mannering knew that she was on the way to the extension in the hall.

"Police are quick, everywhere," Bristow said, with a mild sarcasm. "But you have your points. The Marquis de Cironde et Bles had two daughters. One died at seventeen, the other at twenty-six. The elder one left a widower named Bernard de Lille. Lille wasn't in the Marquis social sphere, and there was some family estrangement. There are pictures of the whole family, including this Bernard de Lille, in a book called *Famous Families of the Loire*. There's a British edition, so it should be at the British Museum, even if it's unobtainable anywhere else."

"Well, well," said Mannering, very softly. "So now we know that Bernard Lisle could have had some moral claim to an interest to the Fioras. He might even have told Francesca the truth—that the cross were her mother's."

"He might have decided that he ought to steal them back," said Bristow dryly. "I can't find any evidence that he was wealthy enough to buy them. How's the girl?"

"Lorna gave her some pheno-barbitone."

"Good idea," agreed Bristow, "but when she comes round, try to make her talk. I'm not sure she's told us everything, and she might talk more freely with you."

"We all have our uses," Mannering murmured. "I'll try."

He rang off.

Ethel called joyfully: "Everything's ready, mum!"

They went into the dining-room. Hungry though he was, Mannering ate mechanically; he said very little.

Lorna faded into the background, a trick she had. Faint sounds of singing came from the kitchen; so at least Ethel was happy.

Mannering said abruptly: "Why did they want to kill Francesca? Why wasn't it enough to rob her? What happened in that hour we can't account for?"

He jumped up, and went out. Lorna waited, looking at his nearly empty plate, guessing the burden on his mind; and guessing where he had gone.

He stood looking down at Francesca Lisle.

She lay on her back, sleeping very quietly, her lips and breast hardly moving. Lorna had drawn the curtains, and the half-light added to her beauty. Bristow wasn't sure the girl had told everything she could, and Mannering was equally doubtful but—did she know the significance of everything she knew? Did she herself know why these men had tried to kill her?

They might try again.

He raised his head, sharply, then went to the window, which overlooked Green Street. Some distance along sat a man in a small open tourer; one of Bristow's men. In the other direction, a man and a boy in dungarees—one of them looked like a boy, anyhow—had a manhole cover up, and were spending a lot of time examing whatever mysteries of wires and pipes lay beneath. Bristow was carrying out his job thoroughly; no one would enter the building without being seen.

Would anyone try?

Mannering went out of the bedroom, closing the door quietly. The study door was ajar. He went in here, because the window overlooked the back of the houses in Green Street and yet another bombed site; when one knew where to look, London was still full of these.

Building had started on some small houses on the site; one of the men "working" there was a Yard man.

So Bristow took this and the situation as seriously as anyone could. The real danger would probably come later; when they had kept Francesca safe for a while and weariness set in; or when they grew used to the idea, and were careless. It was absurd to think that there was danger now.

Wasn't it?

Mannering went back into the dining-room. Lorna was squeezing a piece of bread, making it into a little pellet.

"Bristow had a man following us all the way," she said. "I can't believe——"

"It's giving me the creeps," Mannering growled. "There's a quality of horror that gets into the blood. The man in the office, the ruthlessness, Francesca in the morgue——" He sat down heavily. "I must be getting old or soft in the head. What's the pudding?"

"Plum duff," Lorna said.

He was no longer hungry.

He felt as if he were living in a room filled with mist, and that out of the mist expected danger might come at any moment. Yet he could see nothing, had only a sense that danger was near.

Why had they tried to kill Francesca?
Why had they kidnapped Joy?
Who had told them that he had the Fioras?
Where were the other Fioras now?

. . . . .

Mannering was in the study at half-past three, when the telephone bell rang. Lorna had gone out, to see an art dealer who had offered for some of her paintings then being exhibited; Mannering had encouraged her to go. He had talked to Larraby and Trevor, and kept in touch with business. He had checked over everything that had happened, and the four questions remained as insoluble as ever.

Now, the telephone made him start.

"John Mannering here."

"Mannering," said Ephraim Scoby, "I've just had a message from a friend of mine who's had a talk with Simon Lessing. So you didn't take me seriously."

. . . . .

This was Scoby's voice, beyond all doubt. Voice, laconic manner, ability to startle and to surprise. Yet it was a relief to hear him. There was hope that he could swing over to the attack now, and get Scoby worried and uncertain.

Mannering said: "I took you very seriously."

"You know where to take those jewels tonight."

"I shan't take them anywhere."

"You know about Joy——"

"Joy Lessing may be a nice girl," Mannering said. "I don't know her well. I've seen that she's pretty and I'm told she's good. I'll do everything I can to help someone I don't know—*except* lose a fortune. Your offer was chicken-feed, and you know it. Think again. And what I said before—if the girl gets hurt, you'll get named. I'll take that risk."

"So you're greedy," Scoby said softly.

"That's the way it is," Mannering told him. "I'm not easily scared, either."

Now he had stuck his neck out as far as it would go.

The man at the other end of the line actually laughed.

"So you're not easily scared! You have two dicks outside the front door and another at the back, you can't see out of a door for Bristow's men, and you're not scared! But Bristow can't protect you. He can't protect anyone. I'll get you, Mannering, if you don't come across."

Mannering rang off.

He was sweating.

He was still feeling hot at the forehead and neck when Ethel came in to ask whether he were ready for tea. He said yes, as the telephone bell rang again.

"Yes, Ethel, thanks. If the door bell rings, let me answer it, will you?"

"Just as you like, sir." Ethel backed towards the door. "Do you think the young lady in the bedroom would like a cup, too?"

"I'll see if she's asleep still," Mannering said, and then lifted the receiver. "This is John Mannering." He half expected Scoby's voice again, evidence that he was more ready for bad than for good news.

It was Larraby.

"I've just seen Simon Lessing go into a house in St. John's Wood," Larraby said, in his brisker, van-man voice. "He drove from his flat to Lord's, parked the car in a side street, and was met by a young chap with overlong, reddish hair. He fits the description you gave of the man Ringall."

"The address?" Mannering asked softly.

"Ninety-three Forth Road," Larraby told him promptly. "It leads off Wellington Road, not far from the Underground Station. Shall I expect you here soon, sir?"

Mannering paused to consider. Then: "No," he said. "Come away, Josh. Make absolutely sure that you're not followed, that no one from the house knows you've been watching."

"I don't think you need fear that, sir."

"All right. Send Trevor and the others home when you get to the shop. Lock up, and then come straight here. I'll wait until you arrive."

"Right," Larraby said.

Mannering rang off.

There was hardly time to think, before the door bell rang three times, sharply. It was the bell from the street door and a pre-arranged signal; someone was coming up, and the police were warning him. It seemed always the same; nothing at all happening, or too much on the go at the same time. He stood up and went into the hall, hearing sharp footsteps on the stairs—footsteps which were oddly familiar. Yet he stood away from the door when he opened it, as if afraid of sudden violence.

It was Susan Pengelly.

"Gosh!" she exclaimed. "Frightened of *me*?"

Mannering didn't smile, but drew back. She followed him into the hall.

"Terrified," he said dryly.

"Like all men!" She was almost serious.

He led the way towards the study, and Ethel appeared

in the kitchen-door, tea-tray in hand, and then did a complete about turn without rattling a cup, but muttering:

". . . get another cup."

Susan took one quick look round the study. Mannering had a feeling that she recognised the antiquity and the beauty of some of the precious pieces there. She didn't sit down, and it was obvious that she didn't quite know how to start what she had to say.

Then abruptly: "I've had a telephone call from Simon."

Mannering murmured: "So soon?"

"Oh, he didn't apologise or ask me to forgive," she said. "He's terrified. Apparently he's a prisoner in the same place as Joy. He says Joy's all right, but——" She paused, as Ethel came in, clinking the things on the tray. Ethel went out, on a murmured "thanks" from Mannering, and Susan went on as if there had been no interruption: "He doesn't think either of them will be for long."

"What else?" asked Mannering tautly.

"It's the same old story," Susan said. "They want the Fioras, and they're quite sure that you have them."

"What makes them so sure?" he asked, and almost believed she could answer.

Susan Pengelly eyed him in that snake-like way she had, neck twisted round, head perched a little to one side, lips set tightly so that only the slash of lipstick showed, and eyes narrowed so that they looked as if there was shimmering liquid green behind the long, reddish lashes.

"Either you're very good," she said, "or very, very bad. He says he's seen a receipt, on Quinns paper, for every diamond in the Collection." She paused, but Mannering didn't respond, so she went on: "It was taken from Bernard Lisle."

21

A VISIT BY NIGHT

FIVE minutes afterwards Mannering put down the telephone and watched Sue Pengelly as she poured out tea. She had a knack of making herself at home. She had really beautiful legs and hands and arms, it was a shame that she was burdened with quite such a lump of a figure; but it did not seem to trouble her.

"Scotland Yard says that Simon deliberately shook their man off," Mannering told her.

"I wouldn't be surprised," said Susan. "Look how he shook me off! You don't know Simon very well, do you? He gives the impression of being the strong, silent-man type. As a matter of fact, if there were a war he'd almost certainly win the V.C. or something sensational. Simon's all right when he doesn't have to think. Something goes wrong with his metabolism whenever he does. He thinks that he, and he alone, can save Joy These—people—have told him he mustn't go to the police, so he doesn't. They've given him orders, and he's obeyed them. I don't believe he can think—I think he just feels and acts on impulse. Francesca would find him very trying. Even I do!"

"Did he say anything else?" Mannering asked.

"Just that I was to come and tell you this," Susan declared. "There was another man who came on the line afterwards, and said that he was sure you would be interested to know that he could give that receipt to Scotland Yard. And it was undoubtedly signed by you."

Mannering said softly: "Could Scoby be crazy enough to believe that I'd sign my name to a thing that would send me to jail for ten years, even if it didn't hang me?"

"Well," Susan said practically, "he says he has it, and Simon says he's seen it, and they both said you'll be hearing. More tea?"

"Thanks. Did they say anything else?"

"Not another word that mattered," Susan said. "Simon was almost in tears—tears of vexation and despair, of course, not of weakness! He quite forgot the way we'd parted, so at least he realises that I have a forgiving nature. As a matter of fact," Susan Pengelly went on, "I am nothing like so vixenish as I look. Do you mean to say this receipt was forged?"

"It must have been."

"That's one thing about artists like most of us," remarked Susan, "we can imitate handwriting, can't we? This must be good, if it can to fool the man Scoby—did you say Scoby?"

"Yes."

"That's odd. He wouldn't give his real name, would he? I met a man named Scoby in Paris in the summer vac. He was with Francesca's father, who was over there for a few days. Joy saw him when she was sitting outside the Café de Paris, of all places for a penniless art student, on the Madeleine Boulevard."

"What was he like?" Mannering asked very softly.

Susan put her cup down, leaned back with hands on the arms of the chair and her short legs sticking out straight in front of her.

"Find me a piece of paper and a pencil," she ordered.

Mannering found them.

He didn't look at her as she sketched, although probably she would not have noticed had he breathed down her neck. It wasn't more than three minutes before she picked the paper up and handed it to him.

That was Scoby beyond a shadow of doubt.

And Scoby knew—or had known—Bernard Lisle.

Susan said: "I haven't lost the trick, have I?"

"You haven't lost the trick," Mannering agreed fervently. "I don't know whether his real name is Scoby, or——"

The door opened, and Francesca came in.

She looked as if all the blood had drained out of her face. It left her eyes very bright, and they seemed huge. She hadn't put on lipstick that day, and no rouge or powder.

Yet she looked beautiful. She came in steadily, but rather as if she were in a daze.

Ethel was close behind her: "She just wouldn't stay on the bed, sir. If I woke her up I'm sure I'm sorry, but I tried to make her stay there."

"It's all right, Ethel. Hallo, Francesca. Come and have a cup of tea."

"No, thank you," Francesca said. She looked at Susan without seeming surprised to see her here. "Hallo, Susan. I must go to my flat, Mr. Mannering. Will you excuse me?"

"There's no hurry, and you must——"

She looked at him straightly. "I appreciate all you've done to help me," she said carefully. "I really do. But I feel that I must go back to my flat. I can't stay away any longer. I will thank Mrs. Mannering later."

"All right." Mannering dropped all argument. "I'll take you there." He knew that they would be followed. It was only just round the corner, and the Yard men would watch her as closely in her own flat as they would in his. And it would give him more freedom of action. "Is your hat in the other room?"

"Hat? Oh, yes, I forgot." She turned round, a hand at her head, and went out.

Susan muttered something, *sotto voce*: "I didn't think I would ever come to it, but I'm sorry for her."

"You're certainly not as bad as you paint yourself," Mannering said.

"But I couldn't go and look after her," Susan declared. "I'm just not the big-hearted type, I should soon repent being so full of sympathy. Think she'll be all right?"

"Yes."

"John," she said, startling him by the use of his Christian name.

"Yes?"

"Do you really think you've any hope of finding Joy?"

"Yes."

She looked at him for a long time, and didn't speak

again until footsteps sounded just outside the room. Francesca's. Then:

"You're either a rogue," Susan said, "or a genius. I'd better go with Francesca and find out if I've any maternal instinct to spare for her."

"Sue," said Mannering.

"Yes, Johnny?"

"Don't go with her. Someone wants to kill her. If she should die——"

"Gosh!" exclaimed Susan, using the word almost as an oath, "of course, I'm under suspicion!" She held her breath, then expelled it slowly. "All right, I'll go home and wait like a good little she-devil!"

. . . . .

The policewoman opened the door at Francesca's flat. Francesca looked startled at sight of her, and the dazed look faded from her eyes. She didn't speak at first, but when Mannering went into the little sitting-room with her, she said:

"I don't want anyone here with me, except Cissie. Do you know where Cissie is?"

"No, but I expect she'll soon be back,"

"I don't want anyone else here," Francesca insisted. "Please will you send that woman away? I'm tired of the police and questions and being watched. I just want to be alone. Can't you understand?"

"I think I do. I'm not sure that it's wise——"

"*I don't want that woman here!*"

"All right, Francesca," Mannering said gently, "I'll ask the police if they'll take her away. And I'll telephone you. Anything more I can do for the moment?"

"No," she said quickly, and then moved towards him and touched his hand. Her eyes looked huge. "Forgive me, I don't mean to be ungrateful. I am *very* grateful, for —for everything. I don't feel as if I'm here, it's as if—as if part of me has been cut away."

"I know," Mannering said, and squeezed her hands. "I won't be long."

A VISIT BY NIGHT

He went out.

The policewoman came to the door with him.

"Don't leave her alone for a minute," Mannering said urgently. "Keep the doors open, and listen if you can't see her. She'll order you to go, but hold on like grim death."

"I will," promised the policewoman. She was a solid-looking forty, her ample white blouse and black tie and skirt giving her a uniformed look. "I won't let her kill herself. She'll soon be over this stage, I think."

"I hope you're right," said Mannering fervently.

. . . . .

"Bill."

"Yes," said Bristow, into the telephone.

"Francesca Lisle's back at her own flat, with your policewoman, who thinks she is waiting for a chance to slash her wrists or kill herself somehow. I couldn't agree more. Your responsibility now."

"I'll see to it."

"Thanks. Another thing. Simon Lessing's vanished. He telephoned Susan Pengelly and said that he was a prisoner, held with Joy. That may be true. I'm going out on a *sortie* tonight, and it might be very useful if the police in the St. John's Wood area were as thick as garden peas in a wet summer, but very modest and retiring. If a few extra patrol cars without the word police showing and with the patrolmen out of uniform happened to be in that part of the world I think it might be useful."

There was a long silence.

In it, Bristow was obviously fighting against the temptation to demand more information; or to call Mannering a fool for taking chances.

Bristow the man won the fight.

"All right," he said.

. . . . .

Lorna was back, and in the study when Mannering telephoned Bristow. As Mannering put the receiver down, she said very slowly, almost hurtfully:

"I suppose it's no use asking you not to go."

"I must go," Mannering said simply.

"Josh Larraby may not be right about that house. Or he may not be right about being unobserved." Lorna was uttering each word with great care, as if it were difficult to select them even in their simplicity. She sat beneath a soft, warm light. Every feature of her face was dear to him; and he could guess the sharpness of the fear which stabbed at her. "Scoby has been very smart, hasn't he? You've said so yourself. Perhaps he didn't slip up like that. Perhaps he meant Larraby to see where the youth went, hoping you would go there tonight."

Mannering moved across to her, put a hand on her arm, and smiled gently.

"I think he did."

"Then surely Bristow——" Lorna began, but didn't finish. She moved her hand, squeezed his, then jumped up, bustling. "All right, I won't argue any more! What time will you be going out?"

"About nine, I think."

"As you are, or—with make-up." She meant: "Or disguised?" When he chose, he could perform a Hollywood *artiste*'s job upon himself, could change his appearance so that in the right light he could even fool Lorna; he had a remarkable record of having fooled the police.

"As I am, tonight," he said.

She caught her breath. "You——" She stopped, and the pressure of her fingers was very tight on his. "You won't go defenceless, will you?"

"No, my sweet."

They looked at each other for a long time; or what seemed a long time. It was seven o'clock. They were alone in the flat, for Ethel was out for the evening. They were alone, and at a time like this their possession of each other was urgent and vital.

"John," she said, "is it really worth it? You hardly know the Lessing girl, and you don't know Francesca well."

A VISIT BY NIGHT

He didn't answer, but slid his arm round her waist, and they went out of the room.

. . . . .

It was dark. The wind off the Thames was becoming so strong that if one listened in the quiet, one could hear it stirring the surface of the tireless river, and could hear the water lapping against the banks. No river traffic moved, few cars sped along the Embankment. Mannering searched the shadows of trees and houses, doorways and corners, but saw no one. He walked past Francesca's flat, and saw a light in the front window. He wondered whether the same policewoman were there, and what was happening between them.

Police were watching the flat.

No one watched or followed him.

He walked briskly towards the main road, reached it and had the luck he wanted; a taxi appeared with its sign lighted. It swung into the kerb when he beckoned. He relaxed in the corner, lit a cigarette, then carefully checked all the things he had brought with him. Deliberation and careful planning were a prequisite of success.

One 32 automatic, fully loaded; one extra clip of ammunition—he had a licence; one innocent-looking cigarette-lighter-gun—no licence.

One small, extremely selective tool-kit, was wound about his waist. It restricted freedom of movement a little, but whenever he needed full freedom he could nip the kit off and tuck it into a pocket. The tools were all beautifully hinged—saws, hack-saw, chisel, screw-driver, jemmy—this last in the form of a very thick cold chisel hinged in two places. There was blind cord; thin rubber gloves which stretched skin tight, for quick use; adhesive plaster for his finger-tips; four phials of ammonia for use in emergency, a hammer, a glass-cutter of the latest pattern—these and everything else that a burglar could desire, even if he were masquerading under the soubriquet of "cracksman".

The tools were comparatively new; the technique of using them was of the days of the Baron.

At times it was necessary for him to use the make-up, when a burglary might lead him to the magistrates' court, the Old Bailey and Dartmoor or its equivalent. There was no such risk today, for there would be no come-back from the police. The risk was far greater from Ephraim Scoby and his evil men.

Larraby might have been fooled.

If he had been, then Scoby was probably expecting Mannering to make a bold effort to break in, trying to rescue Joy and Simon Lessing. If one followed the newspapers, that was the kind of thing that Mannering was likely to do. Letting him know where the prisoners were— even letting him think that he knew—was the surest bait known to man. If Larraby had been fooled, Scoby was almost certainly waiting for a burglar.

Mannering did not intend to break in anywhere that night. He was more likely to have to break out.

22

93 FORTH ROAD

It was dark in the side streets.

It was dark when one looked across the grimy brick wall surrounding the silenced terraces and the now soft and demure green Lord's; darker when one walked in the shadow of the wall. The lights of traffic seemed very bright and, perhaps because of Mannering's mood, the noise of traffic sounded very subdued.

He did not know which of the passing cars were police cars, or which of the men who walked slowly were detectives in plain clothes. He was quite sure that Bristow would use every available man from the Yard and from the local Division, and be expecting an emergency call. He probably guessed that Mannering had not told him exactly where he was going because a party of police converging too near would have warned Scoby and his men.

Mannering saw the street name at a corner five minutes after paying off his taxi; black on a white enamel nameplate read: *Forth Road*. The road was long and wide. The houses looked tall, dark and narrow, each with a gate, four stone steps and a shallow porch. Street-lamps at every fifty yards broke the darkness, but between each pair was a patch of murky shadow where men might lurk unseen.

Lighted windows stretched away into the distance, too; curtained, yellow, yet helpful.

A semicircular fanlight showed creamy white, the black number on it was 108; and against it fluttered a big moth. It reminded Mannering of the body in the morgue, the birthmark and Francesca's cold, clutching fingers.

He walked briskly.

He passed a man who stood by the gate of the house. Although Mannering was on the look-out for such a man, it came as a shock. His heart began to beat faster. The man had selected a spot between street-lamps, and where there were no lighted windows or fanlights. He stood quite still. Mannering walked past him, and didn't glance over his shoulder. He didn't need to, for the man began to walk after him.

He saw another man, on the other side of the road.

He had to cross the road to reach Number 93. He crossed. He knew that he could just be seen, but didn't know whether to expect an attack.

Number 93 had a dimly lit fanlight.

He did not hesitate, but turned into the gate. It was of wrought iron, and squeaked. He mounted the four steps and waited on the porch until it had stopped squeaking, knowing full well that he could be seen from the fanlight.

He heard no sound of movement.

At least they were not planning to attack until they knew what he was going to do.

He took out a pencil pocket torch, shone it on the door, found both bell and knocker, banged the knocker and kept his finger on the bell. The knocking made a rude attack on the evening quiet. The bell sounded a long way off.

He stopped knocking and ringing.

Footsteps came from inside the house, but not from behind him. He did not know how close the two men were, but waited.

Scoby opened the door.

. . . . . .

Ephraim Scoby must be obviously very, very sure of himself. Either that, or he had a nerve so strong that nothing really worried him. He was here, quite brazenly. The silent, watching men told Mannering that he had been expected; or that someone had been. Scoby could not be sure that Mannering had not told the police, but behaved as if there were no risk of any kind.

He smiled without parting his lips.

"So Larraby told you." He stood aside, and called softly, throwing his voice beyond Mannering into the street. "Keep your eyes skinned, Charley."

"*Okay,*" floated back.

"Come in," Scoby said. He closed the door when Mannering stepped into a hall about four feet wide. It was dimly lit, the bare walls were papered with imitation oak panelling. "You didn't give the police this address, did you?"

"Nervous?" asked Mannering.

"You'd better hope you didn't give the police this address," Scoby said, "and you'd better tell me the truth, Mannering. Because if I'm in any doubt, I'm going to telephone Bristow. Bristow always acts fast when he gets a telephone message from me. This time, I should tell him to go to Quinns. You know, that curio shop in Mayfair, where everything costs twelve times the price it would in Golders Green. I should tell him to look in three places, pal. The second right-hand drawer of the Sheraton dressing-table in the main show-room; in the vizor of the coat of chain mail which has a bloodstain visible after seven hundred years; and in a little African bronze head, the top of which can be unscrewed. Do you know what he would find there, Mannering?"

Mannering said: "I can guess." His heart was beginning to pound.

"You'd probably guess right," sneered Scoby. "Hot stuff, Mannering, as hot as it comes. There was a job done out at Hampstead last week. By a bit of bad luck, the man whose house was burgled came home at the wrong time, and he got his. The killer got scared and unloaded quick, and I picked it up for a song. I had a man playing customer in Quinns this afternoon, and another to attract the second assistant. Then I made a telephone call. The stuff was planted on you then." Scoby paused, as if to make sure that the facts and all the implications had sunk in, then snapped: "Police know you've come?"

"No," said Mannering.

"You'd better be right. Let's go in here."

Scoby didn't have to open a door, for a man whom Mannering hadn't seen before was standing by it, and opened it for him. It was almost opposite the foot of the stairs. A long passage led alongside the stairs, and there was a light at the far end. There was a light at the landing, too. Another man stood up there, looking down. He didn't speak. Scoby had studied the psychology of nervous pressure and had this all nicely planned. Mannering, whose nerve was as strong as the next man's, could not keep down the pounding at his heart.

"So if the police turn up, they get the news about Quinns," Scoby went on. "You want to know something, Mannering?"

He pushed the door wider open. The watching man just stood and stared at Mannering, balefully. He looked like a cretin, and carried a hammer. He didn't say a word. Mannering went in—and it was like walking into a brick wall in the darkness.

Simon Lessing was in here.

It had been possible from the beginning to sense the evil in these men; to know, from the moment when Francesca's body had been found floating sluggishly in a foot of water, that they were deadly.

Simon was stripped to the waist. There were at least three burn scars on his chest, and a smear of blood on his shoulders. He was sitting on an upright chair, with rope round his waist and ankles, and his arms tied behind him. Sweat glistened on his forehead. His crisp brown hair looked as if someone had pulled him along the ground by it. But he was breathing evenly, and there was defiance in his eyes.

Mannering realised then how well Susan knew Simon Lessing.

The room was long and narrow, had a table and several upright chairs, two easy-chairs, and in the far corner, a window shuttered from the inside with wooden boards.

Scoby grinned one-sidedly.

"I don't think you could take what Lessing's taken," he said, "but maybe you'll have the sense not to make us find out." He made one of those deliberate pauses. Then: "I want you to understand one thing. I'm going all the way. I'm not interested in half-measures. I had those Fioras for four years, and I hadn't been able to cash in on them yet. I killed the old fool who had them to sell, and I've killed and will kill again to make sure I get them back. If I lose, I lose. I know what the stakes are. I knew there was a risk that you'd bring the police tonight, but I'm a gambler, Mannering, and I gambled that you wouldn't. You're a sentimental fool over women. I've been studying you and your record ever since I knew that Lisle was working with you."

Mannering said: "You tried to scare me by putting the police on to me. Where do you think that could get you?"

"So you don't know." The handsome face was set in a sneer. "I know your kind, Mannering. You've got the Fioras. With the police after you, you have to get rid of them quick. And you will. I've got your signature on that receipt, *and* it isn't forged." The sneer became a grin. "You gave a pal of mine a signature on a statement he'd made, days ago. The statement was written in ink that faded, and the details of the Fioras were written in afterwards. I cover everything, don't I?"

Mannering said: "You're still wrong. I haven't the Fioras. What makes you think I have?"

"You have them," Scoby said roughly. "I'll tell you something, Mannering. It might help you to grasp the hard facts. I haven't any future in this country. I've got to vanish. It's all laid on. I've been building up another identity in another place, and everything's fixed—except the money. I need the money, and I've a market for the Fioras, cash down. You're in this deal for what you can get out of it, and I'm not a cheap swindler and I'm not a chiseller. I've offered you ten thousand quid, and it's money for old rope. You'd better accept."

He gave that time to sink in, too.

Simon Lessing said: "If I ever get at you, Mannering——"

"Shut up," Scoby said viciously. "Or I'll shut you up. There's just one thing more I want out of you, and when I've got that—*les rideaux*!" It was an odd quirk to drop in the words of French, and his eyes actually smiled. "Listen to the rest, Mannering. I'll pay you a thousand pounds down, to show earnest. If you welsh, I'd smash your head in the way I had Lisle's smashed. The other nine thousand will be handed over in exchange for the Fioras. You can have Lessing's sister at the same time, but you can't have Lessing. He's fixed for *les rideaux*! Only get it clear in your head, it's got to be a quick deal. If you don't come across—okay, Bristow will have the receipt for the Fioras, he'll find the hot stuff at Quinns, and sooner or later he'll find your body. In this job I win or I lose, and there's no halfway stop."

He meant it.

The man who had followed them in was leaning against the wall, watching.

Lessing gave the impression that he would kill anyone he could reach.

The quiet lasted for a long time before Mannering moved, glanced at Lessing, and then said to Scoby:

"Where's his sister?"

"Upstairs. She's okay."

"When I've seen her I'll believe it."

"Come along up," Scoby said. "Open the door, Mick." The cretin obeyed as if Scoby had control of his reflexes. Scoby gave Lessing another careless glance; but perhaps it was not so careless as it seemed.

"Just think about that one thing, Lessing—did Francesca Lisle tell you anything about this, and how much did she tell you? Don't hold out any longer. Next time you'll really get hurt."

He went out.

The door closed and the cretinous-looking man stood at the foot of the stairs, another on the landing, as Mannering and Scoby went up. Scoby was rubbing his chin; the stubble looked more black than blue.

"I could use a man like Lessing," he said, "but he's too righteous." His grin was sardonic but regretful. "You can pick the honest ones out. But can he take it!" He whistled. "The only thing that made him whimper was a threat to his kid sister, but I don't want to spoil her face for the sake of it. If he won't tell me what Francesca told him, how much she knows, then I'll have to work on little Joy." He talked to Mannering as if to a partner in crime; as if it didn't occur to him that Mannering would gladly have broken his neck.

He stopped at a door. It was locked, and the key was in the outside. Mannering didn't see him signal, but was quite sure that one was given. The man at the head of the stairs moved, slapped Mannering's pockets, felt the automatic and slipped it out as if the pocket were in his own jacket. He slapped Mannering's waist.

"What'n hell——?"

His hands moved swiftly, expertly. He found the clip of the tool-kit, pulled the kit away and held it up. A glint of envy showed in his eyes.

Scoby said: "Mannering, you really do a job, don't you?"

Mannering didn't speak.

The other man slapped his pockets, actually took out the lighter, and dropped it back.

"Okay," he said, "he's harmless now."

"How did you train your experts?" Mannering asked.

"I selected them after they'd been trained," Scoby said. "I got two English, a French, a Pole and an American. They went on the run just before the war ended. If the authorities got them they'd be hanged or shot, so they're glad to work for me. They know this is the last job, and they know they're going to get a big rake-off, so they feel the same as I do about it."

He flung open the door of the room, and strode inside. He didn't get far, but stopped so sharply that Mannering banged into him. Mannering heard a hiss of breath from behind him, the man on the landing saw what had happened. It was glaringly obvious.

The window was wide open, the room was empty. On the floor were some pieces of blind cord, obviously cut.

"It isn't possible," Scoby muttered. "It isn't——" He broke off and swore. Then: "One of you let her go. I'll have his——"

Revelation and opportunity came to Mannering in that moment.

He stepped behind Scoby with a swift, swaying motion, put both hands on his waist, swivelled round with Scoby's feet just off the floor, and pushed him into the man on the landing. The man there tried to dodge, missed a step, then staggered under the full force of Scoby's body.

Mannering didn't wait to see the two men fall, but raced down the stairs.

The cretinous creature crouching at the foot of the stairs, hammer in hand, suddenly became deadly.

In that moment Mannering knew who had smashed Lisle's skull.

23

THE FINAL FEAR OF ALL

THE man crouched, big and powerful, with the hammer raised. He was just the right distance from the bottom tread, too far away for Mannering to jump on to him. Mannering took his hand out of his pocket. Fear was driving him, something that lifted him above the immediate danger from the man waiting here.

His cigarette-lighter flashed.

A tiny bullet caught the cretin on the side of the forehead. It knocked him back. Mannering didn't know whether it went right home or struck a glancing blow. He jumped, and the man reeled back, fingers still clinging to the handle of the hammer. Mannering struck him beneath the chin, heard his teeth snap, knew that he would be out for several minutes.

At least two men were outside in the street.

Two others were upstairs, too, and they wouldn't be there for long.

There might be others in the house.

Mannering flung back the door of Simon Lessing's room. Lessing wrenched at his cords so violently that he dragged the chair inches from the floor and actually stood crouching with the chair jutting out from behind him.

"Joy's gone," Mannering said, and Lessing almost choked. Mannering slammed the door, turned the key in it, grabbed an upright chair and jammed it beneath the handle. He did everything with great precision, hardly looked as if he were in a hurry; the nearness of death calmed instead of panicking him. He took out his knife and cut at Lessing's bonds; only those at the wrists took time. As the rope fell away, Mannering looked at the boarded window.

"Try to move around," he said.

He heard footsteps on the stairs; one set pounding, one

THE FINAL FEAR OF ALL

set staggering. A shoulder hit the outside of the door, and a man grunted. The handle rattled. Mannering reached the boarded window, and pulled a board away. They fitted into slots.

"They'll kill as lief as look at us," he said. "Can you move?" He didn't look round.

"Ye—yes," Lessing gasped. "Sure!"

There was a shot, obviously aimed at the door; and the door sagged. The chair wouldn't hold it for long against the fury of Scoby and his men.

There were those in the street too, remember.

A light flashed in the garden beyond the window. He saw that, then saw another door open at the back of the house. A shadow appeared. Mannering didn't hear anything said and hardly needed to; they were blocking that way out.

He slammed the board back into position.

Lessing was leaning against a table; he was trying with all his strength, but the blood beginning to circulate through his legs and feet was bringing excruciating pain. He couldn't stand properly, there had never been a chance that he could walk out either at the back or the front.

A telephone stood on a wall-bracket near the door.

The door was shivering under the impact of at least two men, and suddenly a different sound came, of a hammer being used against the wooden panels—thick, oak panels. Mannering lifted the receiver, and the buzzing sound came promptly, the line was in order. He dialled, his fingers still and cold.

Outside, Scoby shouted: "Cut that telephone cable!"

"*Nine-nine-nine*," Mannering muttered. It was like an invocation to some god of numbers. There was silence outside, as men stopped hammering at the door; but someone started on the window, and glass smashed beyond the boards.

"*There it is!*" roared Scoby.

"Information Room, Scotland Yard."

"*Ninety-three Forth Road, St. John's Wood, armed raiders.*" Mannering spoke with controlled swiftness. "*Can you*——?.

A shot sounded in the hall, loud in the narrow confines —and the line went dead.

Mannering couldn't be sure whether the Yard had received the message, whether "93 Forth Road" had registered? They were bound to realise which Forth Road.

More glass smashed.

A bullet came through the boards at the window, and the hammering started again at the door.

"Go buy me a gun," Simon Lessing mouthed. He tried to grin. He was actually standing now, but it was obvious that he couldn't take half a dozen steps without falling. "Or a shroud. What does——?"

The door bulged, near the handle and at one panel. They couldn't see through either hole, but it wouldn't be long before they would be able to and before Scoby would shoot. Scoby had meant what he said, he would shoot to kill. He'd played for high stakes, and he meant to exact the full price for his failure.

He would lose, wouldn't he?

Mannering slid his hand into his waist, took out a small phial, and moved towards the door.

"Want to—get it over quick?" Simon gasped. "Gimme —time to apologise."

Mannering said: "Accepted." He reached the door. The head of the hammer leapt in sight as the panel splintered; it was only a matter of seconds now. He held the phial close to the hole; if they fired, he would lose his hand. He flicked the phial through, then jumped away.

There was silence at the window.

From outside, there came a startled, choking cry.

"What the hell——?"

Two men began to splutter.

Simon Lessing listened and watched Mannering intently. He looked as if he had been dragged through a water-mill, then across a spiked board. But there was a light in his eyes and a triumphant grin on his face.

"John Mannering," he said. "You're *good*. You're so——"

He stopped.

THE FINAL FEAR OF ALL

Mannering spun round towards the window.

A police whistle sounded, and it wasn't far away. Lessing raised his hands, the fingers clenched in a kind of supplication; as if hope, which had been taken away from him, had miraculously been brought back.

"We'll find her," he said, fiercely, "they'll never find her now, thank God, thank——"

Outside in the hall, men were coughing and spluttering and staggering away from the door. Outside in the garden, men were shooting; another police whistle sounded.

A car engine roared.

Mannering went to the door, pulled the chair away savagely, ignored Lessing's shout of: "Careful!" and went into the hall. The front door was open, and the headlights of a car flashed past. There was no sign of Scoby. The cretinous man was on the floor, his head battered as Bernard Lisle's had been.

Another car passed.

Scoby was on the run, and the police were after him. Scoby had a fifty-fifty chance of getting away, and if he escaped this time, he might try again.

A uniformed policeman and a man in plain clothes came running. A second car drew up, and the door opened and more men jumped out.

"I'm Mannering," Mannering said, in a terse, hard voice. "We must get a message to the Yard at once. Radio it, please." A man just in front of him was staring into his face. "I tell you I——"

"Okay, it's Mannering," the man said. "What's that?"

"The radio," Mannering said, "call the Yard." He was making his way towards the street. Lessing was staggering after him. Police were watching, momentarily stilled by his manner, although there were footsteps at the back of the house, and men were coming in there.

A policeman picked up the radio-telephone in the front of the car.

"All right, what is it?"

"Watch Riverside Walk and Francesca Lisle's flat," Mannering said. The patrol man repeated the words almost before Mannering had got them out. "Watch Lisle's flat, allow no one in. If Joy Lessing arrives, hold her. Don't let her in, don't let her go, hold her."

". . . don't let her go, hold her," the patrolman repeated into the mouthpiece. A voice came back through the speaker.

"Okay, message received, we'll see to it."

Lessing kept on his feet somehow, swaying. He grabbed Mannering's arm and pulled him round.

"What's got into you? What's this about Joy?"

"Simon," Mannering said in the same terse way, "you might be lucky with Francesca, you might even be lucky with Sue Pengelly, but you drew a bad number with your sister. Sorry. Coming?" He turned to the patrolman. "Can we get to Chelsea in a hurry?"

"Get in."

"Thanks." Mannering bent down, to get in. Lessing didn't move. "If you're coming, now's the time," Mannering said to Simon, then stopped and stared at the radiotelephone; a voice was coming from it, for it was still "live".

"Patrol Car Fifty-two reporting, we've crashed, escaping car a Jaguar, colour grey, last seen heading for Marble Arch. Keep a sharp look-out, the driver is armed. Patrol Car Fifty-two . . ."

Lessing was getting into the patrol car. He didn't speak. Nor did the patrolman who took the wheel or the other who slid in next to him.

They moved along the street at speed.

Front doors were open, windows were up, people were at their gates, clear in the garish brightness that had come to Forth Road. Tyres squealed. Once they were round the corner, the driver switched on his headlights.

Simon Lessing growled: "Tell me what you mean."

"All right, Si," Mannering said, very quietly. "One of the most puzzling questions was—why kidnap Joy? Was it to bring pressure to bear on me? They might try that incidentally, but it wasn't likely to be the main reason. The only answer I could see at first was this: Joy knew something dangerous to Scoby, or was believed to. What

THE FINAL FEAR OF ALL 171

dangerous knowledge could she have? Then there was another angle. Why had Scoby only kidnapped Joy, although he'd tried to murder Francesca? Why treat the two girls so differently? Thinking about both girls made one thing show up clearly. Joy disappeared immediately it was known that Francesca *wasn't* dead. It wasn't long before I asked myself whether Francesca knew something that could be dangerous *to* Joy? Or at least—did Joy have reason to think she did?

"Then it came out that Joy knew Scoby—they'd met in Paris. Could she have been spying on Lisle, through Francesca? I kept an open mind about that until I got here. Then I knew the answer."

"What—what made you sure?" Lessing's voice was hoarse.

"Joy's disappearance tonight," Mannering said. "I didn't believe that Scoby would let Joy escape unless he wanted to. He rounded on his men, but they wouldn't cut the cords and let her go—why should they? The cord wasn't frayed or untied. It was there to make me think she'd been a prisoner, and escaped. Scoby had gone to a lot of trouble to lure me to the house. Why? To give evidence that Joy was held here?

"Once I felt sure that Joy was involved—I panicked." Mannering shrugged. "If Joy was kept out of the way because Francesca knew—or might know—the truth about Joy, then Francesca's in acute danger. The Yard knows, she's being guarded, but the one person who would certainly be allowed to get at her is Joy——"

Simon drew in a hissing breath.

The car turned a corner, and threw Simon against Mannering. He felt the youth's hot breath on his cheek, and guessed what Simon was feeling.

Simon grunted: "Go on. I can take it."

"No one would stop Joy from going to see Francesca," Mannering said. "Francesca's in a mood to take her own life, even a little encouragement would send her right over the line; or a poisoned tablet or two. She's ready made for suicide. And——"

Simon muttered: "I don't believe it! Joy wouldn't——"

"Simon," said Mannering, "I honestly believe that Joy believes that Francesca knows that she, Joy, was working with Scoby and others over the Fioras. I think that Joy believes that her only chance of keeping clear of the law is a dead Francesca. I think Joy is the reason for the first attempt to kill Francesca. I think they captured and tortured you to find out if Francesca had told you anything which could incriminate Joy. Sorry."

The car raced on, now on the Embankment and treating it as if it were Donnington Park.

24

THE RETURN OF JOY

FRANCESCA sat in the quiet of her bedroom, the dressing-table and the bedside light on, so that the charming room was very bright; the brightness showed the pallor of her face, and the unnatural brightness of her eyes. She sat with her hands folded in her lap, one moment relaxed, the next gripping tightly.

Close at hand was a razor; the thick, sword-like blade was out of the holder. She turned her hands slowly, and looked at her pale wrists. And she listened. The policewoman and Cissie were in the kitchen, with the door open. This door was closed, but they'd taken the key away. They kept making excuses to come in. They would be in again in a moment, and she would lose the razor; yet in some strange, helpless way, she wasn't able to make herself hide it.

They wouldn't look under the bed, if she put it there.

The razor had been meant for her father's birthday, in a few days' time. A secret to hug to herself and a surprise which would have delighted him.

She found strange fascination in its brightness.

The front-door bell rang.

Convulsively, Francesca moved, snatched up the blade, and thrust it under the bed, pushing the razor and the case after it.

Both Cissie and the policewoman came out of the kitchen. One was at the bedroom door in a second, opening it and peeping in. The other went to the front door. Francesca believed that it was Cissie who looked in.

Then she recognised a voice which made her jump to her feet.

"Where's Miss Lisle?" Joy Lessing cried, as if she were distracted. "Where is she? I must see her."

"Why, that's Miss *Lessing*!" Cissie had been at the bedroom door, but she moved quickly away from it. "So you're all right! You're not—— *Oh*!"

"Where is she?" Joy's shrill voice was nearer.

"She's in—she's in the bedroom, Miss Joy! But don't go upsetting her any more, she——"

"It's all right, Joy," said Francesca, opening the door wide. "I'm all right. I'm so glad you're back."

The policewoman and Cissie seemed to fade into the background. Joy, with her back to the closed front door, and Francesca, outlined against the bright lights of her own room, stood and looked at each other.

Joy's eyes were searching, but she looked dreadful. She had on no make-up, her hair was dishevelled, a scratch over her right eye was bleeding, and there was a smear of blood on her chin.

Joy's searching gaze lost something of its brightness. They both moved, as if compelled by a force they didn't understand, and held each other tightly. Joy was sobbing, Francesca crying silently. Cissie couldn't stand it any longer; she turned away with a catch in her breath. The policewoman was tougher, but her eyes had a very bright sheen.

"Cissie," she said, "go and make some tea."

Cissie sniffed, and went off.

The quiet words seemed to affect the two friends. They

drew back from each other, and turned towards the bedroom. Francesca went in first. Joy closed the door, pushing it so that it slammed. The policewoman didn't open it, believing there was nothing to fear with someone else with the girl. She went into the kitchen, where Cissie was blowing her nose.

"This might be the very thing she needs," the policewoman said. "Better leave them for ten minutes or so, before we interrupt." She took a packet of cigarettes from the dresser, lit one, and then said: "I'd better report that Joy Lessing's back. She looks as if she's had a rough time, doesn't she?"

"She looked *awful*," Cissie muttered, and then flashed irritably: "I wish you wouldn't puff that smoke all over my face."

"Sorry. Keep your hair on." The policewoman, now looking completely relaxed, went into the hall. The telephone was in the living-room, in sight. She heard a reassuring murmur of voices from the bedroom.

She went to the telephone.

· · · · · ·

"Oh, it's been dreadful," Francesca said. "Did you—did you know about—Daddy?" It was the first time she had mentioned her father. Something in Joy's coming had helped her, she was able to speak without breaking into tears.

"I couldn't believe it," Joy said, "I just couldn't believe it, darling. Knowing how you loved him——"

Francesca caught her breath.

"I can't tell you how worried I've been," Joy said. "Especially after his letter to you. It must have——"

Francesca exclaimed: "What letter? Joy, what do you mean?"

"Don't you *know*?" breathed Joy. Her pretty features were oddly set, her eyes hard and clear. It was as if she were looking for something which she expected to find.

Gradually relief crept into her eyes; into her manner.

"Oh, my dear," she said, "I hate to tell you." She

paused again, and moistened her lips. She saw the horror in Francesca's eyes, as if the truth were dawning on Francesca. "You—you loved him so much, I know, but——"

"Joy, what is it? Tell me!" Francesca stood absolutely motionless. "Don't spare my feelings."

"But—but it's so cruel," Joy whispered, and there was a catch in her breath. "I was—I was taken prisoner, the men were brutes. *Beasts!*" She paused, as if she could not force herself to go on, the memory was too horrible. How was Francesca to know that she was improvising with desperate speed, seeking something plausible, seeking the thing which would drive her to the final point of desperation; to death by her own hand. "They—they told me what it was all about. Your father—Franky, darling, I hate saying it, but he was one of *them*. He worked with them, then stole these jewels from them. They were fighting each other. He—he knew they knew the jewels were here, that's why he sent for them. He didn't mind risking even your life, Franky, but you can forgive him, he was so desperate, so——" She broke off, choking.

Francesca looked as if she could not move.

"I hate myself for telling you, but you've got to know," Joy went on, with fierce intensity. "He was there when the men attacked you and took the jewels from them, and he took them back. But he couldn't get away. They went after him. He wrote a letter to you, before they killed him. *Didn't* you get it?"

The question came abruptly, almost fiercely, but Francesca did not notice that.

"No. No—Oh!" Her eyes grew large. "There *was* a letter. I had it with me when I went out to—to see Daddy. I just put it in my pocket."

Joy said swiftly: "Which coat?"

"I—I haven't got it now. It was in the river, and——"

"Oh, there," said Joy, and turned away, to hide the fierce light of her relief. Then she went on: "He told his—his friends that he'd written to explain everything, to ask you to forgive him. He thought he would be able to escape, but knew he dared not come back. That's everything.

Oh, Franky darling! If only I could help in some way, *any* way."

Francesca stood with her eyes almost closed, as if she hadn't heard. But she had. She opened her eyes slowly and said:

"You can help me, Joy."

"Oh, darling, just tell me how!"

"Go—go and talk to Cissie and the other woman, the policewoman," Francesca said. "Tell them I must rest, I can't bear to talk to anyone for a while. Will you—will you keep them away?"

"Well, yes, of course," said Joy. "But how will that help?"

"Joy, please, don't argue!"

"Well, all right," Joy said, and felt completely triumphant. She hesitated, turned away, and then went out. She looked back once, then closed the door. She could hear radio music from the kitchen; the maid and the policewoman were in there. She stood by the door.

She heard the bedroom window open.

She waited.

. . . . .

Francesca opened the window slowly and deliberately. Outside, there was a small balcony. The obsession to kill herself, was so great that she didn't think of anyone who might be waiting outside. In fact, a Yard man was there.

He didn't look up.

Francesca went nearer to the edge of the balcony. This was the third floor, and it was a long drop. The river was dark, and there were no stars, the only light came from the street-lamps and the room behind her.

Suddenly, noise broke the quiet. Tyres screamed. Cars swung into sight, one from either corner. Francesca knew they were converging on here. She did not know why, she only realised that unless she jumped soon, they would stop her from going to join her father.

She stepped up on to the balcony. The man in the street

was looking at the approaching cars. Francesca raised her arms, ready to dive on the the stone below.

She didn't notice the shadow behind her. She didn't hear the furtive movements, because of the cars below. She swayed. It wasn't so easy, something seemed to be drawing her back. She actually swayed backwards, then gritted her teeth—and sprang.

A hand grabbed her dress.

Francesca fell, but didn't go far. The hand clutched her tightly. She kicked and struck out blindly, but all she did was to scratch her hands and stub her toes. She was dragged back remorselessly, hearing a voice which sounded like Cissie's, then heard a scream.

She felt herself lifted back on to the balcony, then half-dragged and half-carried towards the window. The light was bright.

"Let me go," she sobbed, "let me go. I want to die! *I want to die!*"

The policewoman said: "All right, dear, just take it easy." She hoisted her through into the bedroom, where Cissie was standing, with the door wide open. Joy wasn't here.

"Make her let me go!" sobbed Francesca.

"She's gone," Cissie cried, but she wasn't talking to Francesca. "I couldn't stop her, she *kicked* me and ran away."

"All right," the policewoman said. "They'll catch her down below."

But they didn't catch Joy Lessing.

She appeared in the hall as the police came in, two of them in the lead. The tenant of the downstairs flat had opened the door for them, and her flat door was open. Joy rushed into the flat, slammed the door, ran into the front room; it was in darkness. She reached the window and flung it up, and was climbing out before the police had time to reach her.

She raced across the Embankment towards the river. Men were ten yards behind her when two more police cars came screeching up. One man risked his life and darted over to the far pavement. By that time, Joy had reached the parapet and was standing on it, poised to dive. The river was high, and few lights shimmered on the black, oily-looking surface.

Joy Lessing dived in.

By the time the policeman had reached the parapet, she was twenty yards away, swimming strongly. The first policemen didn't go in; two men did, but their heavy serge uniforms were sodden in a moment, they hadn't a hope of catching her. She seemed to be swimming strongly towards the other side.

By radio and telephone, the police in Battersea and Lambeth, Chelsea and Fulham, were all alerted, and the River Police were told. On duty near Lambeth Bridge, not so far down river, was Sergeant Worraby.

. . . . .

"If she was swimming, it doesn't help to know where she went in," said Sergeant Worraby, "but if she went under pretty quickly, she'll be over by Rickaby's Wharf, south side. If she banged her head against those barges moored opposite the Battersea Power Station, she would fetch up at that little beach near the Fun Fair. You know. But we'd better keep a sharp look-out everywhere. Swimming strongly, they said."

"Wonder why she jumped in?" said Jem Norton musingly.

"Caw strewth, you and your ruddy questions," grumbled Worraby. "Never stop, do they? Worse'n my kids, before they grew up. At least they did grow up!"

Norton fell silent for fully three minutes. Then:

"Blowing a bit," he said. "Think it's going to rain?"

Worraby scarcely breathed an answer; he didn't care if it rained or snowed.

They didn't say anything for ten minutes or more. By then they were approaching the Power Station, belching smoke which was dimly visible against the sky, whitey-grey on black.

"*What's that?*" Norton cried, and the searchlight swivelled round and fell upon a policeman's helmet. Worraby, in a good temper again, fished it in. As he did so, something slid from the side of the launch to his feet. He picked it up. It was a letter, once sodden but now dry. It was curved round to the shape of the boat-hook, which had kept it in position and out of sight.

He peered at it.

"Miss F. Lisle," he read aloud. "Lisle! Blimey! Jem—it's that letter we took out of the coat last week."

. . . . .

They turned and started down river, completed the run three times, and sent in negative reports until Worraby decided that there was only one likely place left, unless the girl was still swimming. He had the letter in his pocket, still unopened.

"If she got as far as Lambeth Bridge, she'd fetch up near the Festival Hall steps. You know, where that Lisle girl was, Monday." He kept his sharp look-out as they neared the Festival Hall, helped by the floodlit buildings on the other side.

"Hold it!" Worraby called suddenly. He peered at the water where it shimmered under the light of the searchlight. "There she is," he said. "Hard astern, get me in the other side."

Five minutes later, Joy Lessing's body was aboard. Worraby was bending over her.

"Jem."

"Yeh, sarge?"

"Radio back, will you? Say we found her, and I'm trying A.R. but I'm not hopeful. Nasty gash in her forehead where she hit something. I reckon she was kept down under them barges, and didn't have a chance. Okay, okay, get on the 'phone, I'll look after her. And cut out the sleeping-beauty muck, too."

"Okay," Jem said, but didn't move. "Sarge."

"Yeh?"

"Think we gotta hand in that letter? You'll get the kicks for it being on board, and——"

"Listen, Jem," Sergeant Worraby said in an unexpectedly mild voice, "we slipped up, and we'll say so."

He looked at the letter again.

25

THE LOVE OF FRANCESCA

A POLICE-SURGEON gave Francesca a needle of morphia, which was both wise and kind, and she was taken from her flat to a nursing home, unaware of what was happening.

Before then she had told the police and Mannering what Joy had said, as if she wanted to make them understand why she had to die.

Mannering went to the Green Street flat.

Lorna was in his study; she always waited there when he was out on an errand from which he might not come back.

He told her, quietly, finished the story about Simon Lessing, and went on:

"Scoby had to find out how much Francesca knew, had to let Joy talk to Francesca. They couldn't understand why Joy hadn't been named to the police, because they were sure Francesca knew about Joy. The policewoman at Riverside Walk heard some talk about a letter which Francesca didn't get. There's a missing clue. I don't suppose it will matter much, unless——" He broke off.

"Unless what?" All the strain had gone from Lorna's face, making her look years younger.

"Unless it tells us where the Fioras are," Mannering said. He gave a wide grin. "I told Bristow about the jewels Scoby planted at Quinns, there won't be any complications about that." He scowled, as suddenly as he had smiled. "I wonder if they picked up Scoby, or any of his men."

"Bristow will tell you soon," Lorna said. "Don't worry any more. Francesca's safe, and Joy——" She didn't finish.

Mannering managed to scoff at her. "Feel strong enough to pour me out a whisky-and-soda?" he asked. "I think I could sit back and relax."

In fact, he felt like prowling, but it wouldn't help. The telephone bell didn't ring. He fought against the desire to telephone Bristow, who would probably be out and about.

Then the front-door bell rang, and he couldn't get to it quickly enough, was actually touching the handle when Lorna exclaimed:

"Be careful! It might be——"

"It's Bristow," Bristow called, in a voice which no one was ever likely to imitate successfully.

He looked tired, but also looked content. He allowed himself the luxury of a yawn and the satisfaction of a whisky-and-soda and one of Mannering's cigarettes. When he'd lit that, he said:

"Talking of cigarettes, we found Virginia One's at Scoby's place in Forth Street, and the cotton-wool was the same kind that you found. One of his shoes fits our plaster cast, too. But that's by the way. We got him in Soho. He tried to kill himself, but he'll live to hang." Bristow drew on his cigarette, refreshed himself with a drink, then went on with a glint in his eyes: "Next time anyone talks to me about abolishing capital punishment, I'll tell them the story of Ephraim Scoby. He's called himself that for a long time, but had another identity—he's M'sieu Boutelle of Neuilly, near Paris. We found all that out. We also know the story. I came straight here because I thought you deserved to hear it. It's really quite simple."

He sipped and smoked again.

Mannering was both grateful and patient.

"Lisle, or Bernard de Lille, was the son-in-law of the Marquis de Cironde et Bles," Bristow went on abruptly. "We knew about that. He had met the family when valuing some jewels, for he was a jewel merchant, and married the Marquis's daughter, much against parental wishes. So the Marquis cut them off, and his daughter, Lisle's wife, died without seeing her parents again.

"Later, there was the fire, and need for the Marquis to sell the jewels. We know that the dealer he used was killed for them.

"After all that, Bernard Lisle had an idea. He'd felt bitterly that his daughter Francesca wasn't getting her true birthright, and he decided to try to put that right. When he told her the cross was her mother's he really meant that it should have been.

"After hearing about the theft of the Fioras, he started a search for them. Being in the trade, that wasn't impossible. He got as far as Scoby, was sure that Scoby either had the jewels or knew where they were. He waited until Scoby began to explore the market, then nipped in and stole them—from Scoby's Neuilly house."

Bristow paused, to sip his drink.

Mannering was smiling faintly, Lorna was sitting on a pouf with her head against his knees.

"I needed that whisky," said Bristow, looking in surprise at his empty glass. The decanter was by his side.

"Help yourself," said Mannering.

"Oh, may I? Thanks." Bristow replenished it quickly. "Well, that was the background. At the time he stole the Fioras back, Lisle considered that he had a moral right to them—or Francesca had. He took some other stuff from Scoby too, and sold it; that's how he came into a fortune, and was able to move to the Chelsea flat.

"But Scoby was after him.

"Scoby had lived on and off in France, where he planned to retire as M. Boutelle. London was bound to get too hot for him soon. He planned to marry Joy and retire, and he needed the Fioras badly. They were worth a hundred thousand pounds on any market, and he had a collector who was prepared to buy without asking questions. That collector's a man we'll watch.

"Well, Scoby went after Bernard Lisle.

"Joy Lessing helped him gladly. He and she met in Paris on one of her student painting holidays. I don't pretend to know what got into her, but the facts speak for themselves. It wasn't just infatuation for Scoby, but went much deeper. Anyway, Joy spied on Lisle. Scoby tried a bit of blackmail—saying that anyone with the Fioras would be suspected of the original murder. And Lisle had actually sold stolen jewels—that could be proved. So Lisle couldn't ask for police help. In the long run that single fact killed him," Bristow declared solemnly, and sipped.

"He found out he was followed," the Yard man went on, "on the morning of Francesca's birthday. He was cornered by the man Ringall. Under pressure, John, he said he'd given you the Fioras."

Mannering didn't speak.

"But why should he?" asked Lorna.

"He wanted to convince the others that they weren't at the flat, so made up a plausible story—that you were a high-class fence. Other people think so, too. He'd known of you, for years. He'd been nervous about Francesca's friendship with you, because of your reputation as Hawkeye." Bristow allowed himself a grin. "He wouldn't have worried if he'd known as much about you as I do! Anyhow, Scoby was quite ready to believe you were a fence—he must have known a thing or two."

"I'm in a charitable mood, Bill," Mannering said. "I forgive you that *canard*."

"But if Scoby believed John had the collection," Lorna put in quickly. "Why should he go after Francesca when her father telephoned her?"

Bristow put out one cigarette and lit another.

"As Lisle's dead, we can't be absolutely sure," he said. "But when a man is as scared as Lisle was, he'll do odd things and take odd chances. He telephoned Francesca, as you know. He thought he'd shaken Scoby and Co. off—but hadn't. He hoped to get to the Festival Hall Terrace in time to collect the jewels from Francesca and send her away safely. Again—he didn't.

"In a despairing effort to keep Francesca out of trouble, he made a fatal mistake. He knew Joy Lessing was involved, and warned Francesca in a letter sent by special delivery. The mistake could only have been made when he knew himself to be absolutely cornered, and almost crazy. To save himself, he told Joy that he'd sent this letter."

Bristow paused, and Mannering said musingly:

"I'm catching on, now."

"It all adds up," Bristow declared, almost smugly. "Scoby was really scared by then. He had to make sure Francesca couldn't talk. You know how he tried to. He didn't know that she had never opened the letter."

"I can't understand why she didn't," Lorna put in.

"She didn't know who it was from," Bristow explained. "It wasn't addressed in her father's hand, but on a typewriter. There had been several telegrams of apology from guests who couldn't come. Francesca was very much on edge, and—well anyway, she didn't open it, because it's been found, the seal unbroken."

Lorna didn't comment.

"Dare we ask where?" Mannering ventured mildly.

"That's a trade secret," Bristow said. "The whole thing turned on the letter and Joy Lessing's part in the plot, of course. If Joy's part were known, the police would be after her at once, she and Scoby would be for it. It's an odd fact," went on Bristow, "that Scoby was more scared by danger to Joy than to himself. He'd his other identity all prepared, of course, and she hadn't. He was to go to Paris and wipe out all traces he'd left in England, and in a few weeks Joy was to join him. If suspicion was aroused against Joy, it could have led to disaster. So he had to make sure she was out of reach of the police.

"You know how he did that," Bristow went on, "and you know why. The final move was brilliant in its way. Joy knew how Francesca doted on her father, and thought it possible to drive Francesca to suicide. With Lisle's daughter dead, there was no risk that anything her father had said in the past would be remembered, and implicate Joy."

Bristow smoothed down his hair.

"Well, you know what they did," he went on. "You

know, or guess, that they were afraid that if Francesca knew about Joy, she might have told Simon. That's why they kidnapped him."

"But you don't know why Lisle went back to his office, and——"

"Whoa back," interrupted Mannering. "We don't know a lot of things. Why did Lisle give Francesca that cross, in the first place?"

"He thought it was safe enough," Bristow declared. "I can't answer for his reasoning or his frame of mind. Sentiment on Francesca's twenty-first might have had something to do with it. There are some things I can tell you——"

"About what happened on the Festival Hall Terrace, I hope," Mannering said dryly.

"Oh, yes. There was an unknown third party present," Bristow told him, with almost ponderous deliberation. "By name——"

"Abe Prinny," murmured Mannering.

Bristow looked almost sour.

"So you did know."

"I guessed."

"You probably knew all the time," agreed Bristow. "Prinny had been offered the jewels by Lisle. They were too big for him, but he looked for a market. Then he discovered the kind of trouble Lisle was in. So he also followed Lisle to Waterloo, and when Scoby had the jewels, Prinny crept up in the dark, and snatched them.

"He wasn't recognised, but he was suspected. Scoby went to see him next day. Prinny said Lisle had left the cross with him, as evidence that he—Lisle—had the collection. Scoby wasn't satisfied. Prinny, as you know, was terrified by then. Next we had a squeal from someone who owed Prinny a grudge, and who heard him and Lisle talking. You know what happened. Prinny tried to save himself by naming you, John; you'd been there, and Scoby'd brought you in, too. After we let Prinny go, Scoby's men saw him, he confessed he'd taken the jewels, and—again to save himself—said he'd given them to you.

"That was what Scoby was ready to believe, but it didn't save Prinny."

There was a short silence before Bristow went on: "Well, that's that.

"Now for Lisle.

"Lisle didn't know what had happened after he'd been knocked out at the Terrace. He came round and rang his flat. A man answered. He guessed it was a policeman, and daren't go there. He'd nowhere to go, so he went to his office. He had to sooner or later, because his passport was there, and money he needed badly. He'd arranged to see Prinny there, too, but Prinny didn't turn up.

"Instead, Scoby's men were waiting. Because Lisle could name Joy, he was killed."

Mannering shifted his position, and Bristow paused almost expectantly.

"Who told you he was dead?" Mannering asked. "You had a squeal, didn't you?"

"One of the odd things that happen, John," Bristow said. "It was Prinny's wife. She went to keep the appointment instead of Prinny, saw Scoby's men leave, and heard them talking. So she rang the Yard."

Mannering said: "I see, Bill," very quietly.

"I just don't understand about the letter," Lorna said. "Francesca was worried because her father was missing, and——"

"It arrived during the party. Cissie the maid gave it to her just as she was leaving to go to Waterloo. She didn't dream it was from Lisle, who hadn't mentioned it. She had plenty to worry about, and put it in her pocket. It was actually found in the coat pocket taken out of the Thames by the river patrol that night. The other things were handed over, but the letter was dropped and accidentally tucked aside. It was found tonight, when the sergeant in charge used the boat-hook for the first time since Monday. The letter was typewritten and quite legible, and it tells the whole story."

Mannering didn't even say: "Trade secret?"

"You'd better have another drink," Lorna said to Bristow.

* * * * *

It had been a glorious spring; so glorious that the pessimists were already worrying about the bad summer which was sure to follow. And much had happened. Francesca was herself again, and yet not herself, being remote and withdrawn. Simon was her constant companion, but obviously did not know how he stood with her.

Susan Pengelly remained her usual self. Lorna frequently said she wanted to paint the girl, but couldn't bring herself to ask her to sit.

It was just before dark one evening when Francesca called on the Mannerings, and after a few hesitant minutes told them that she was going to France.

"My father was born there," she said, "my mother was French, and I feel that I'd like to live there for a while. There is a little money and some property, all mine now. I shall go very soon and only one thing worries me."

"What's that?" Mannering asked.

She looked so very beautiful; and remotely sad.

"Simon is the worry," she said. "I don't want to hurt him, but I am not in love. I shall never be able to marry him. I've told him what I'm going to do, and he talks wildly about coming and living in France near me. Can you—can you think of a way to stop him?"

Mannering and Lorna were very quiet, before Lorna said:

"Have you told Simon you can't even think of marriage?"

"Not—not in so many words."

"He'll only believe it from you," Lorna said, "shall I telephone him, and ask him to come here?"

Francesca said: "Will you, please? It will help so much to have you near."

* * * * *

Francesca and Simon were in the drawing-room, alone, for a long time. Mannering wasn't quite sure how long.

He was glad that it was at least twenty minutes, for that gave Susan Pengelly time to arrive. Mannering had telephoned her, suggested that she should come, and warned her that when Simon left he would probably be in an execrable mood. She was outside, sitting in Simon's Triumph.

"I can take it," she had said. Mannering remembered her pause and her little laugh as she had gone on: "We can't all have your wife's matrimonial judgment."

"And that reminds me," Mannering had said, "my wife won't be happy until she's painted you. She's wanted to ever since——"

"Granted, if she'll take a risk afterwards, and let you sit for me," Susan had said. "You'll make a lovely devil."

THE END

THE BARON AND THE ARROGANT ARTIST

JOHN CREASEY

The young man was both rude and arrogant—but what kind of excuse was that for trying to kill him?

When an unpleasant young man called Forrester forced his way into Quinns, determined that Mannering should finance his artistic efforts, the art dealer was firm but unimpressed.

The Baron was not to know that later that day he would receive a desperate phone call from the artist's terrified girl-friend. She had found Forrester half-dead, hanging with a noose round his neck. But why should such a brash young man want to kill himself? Or was he the victim of attempted murder?

'The Baron's career is a crescendo of thrills'
Daily Mail

CORONET BOOKS

ROGER WEST TAKES FLIGHT

John Creasey

Chief Superintendent Roger West of the Yard is known to millions through John Creasey's exciting stories. Relentless in the battle against crime, West always gets his man in the end. In these three gripping full-length novels this London 'copper' leaves his home beat and travels the world on the dangerous trail of master criminals.

'The Roger West stories are perhaps the most successful of all Mr Creasey's output'
The Guardian

'Skilled story-telling, smooth as travel by super-jet, and small, telling details, beautifully observed'
Evening Standard

CORONET BOOKS

HOLIDAY FOR INSPECTOR WEST

John Creasey

Riddel was an unpopular MP—but murder seemed a bit drastic

Inspector Roger West's quiet family holiday at the seaside is interrupted by the news that an MP has been savagely murdered. In spite of his wife's protests, he feels impelled to rush back to London and take charge of the case.

But West was to find that the Jonathan Riddel murder case was far more complicated than he had ever expected. And far more dangerous...

'The Roger West stories are perhaps the most successful of all Mr Creasey's output'
The Guardian

CORONET BOOKS

JOHN CREASEY

The Baron Series
- ☐ 02486 0 The Baron Goes Fast — 30p
- ☐ 18305 5 Sport for the Baron — 30p
- ☐ 18763 8 The Baron and the Arrogant Artist — 35p
- ☐ 19865 6 The Baron Goes A-Buying — 40p

Inspector West Series
- ☐ 17845 0 Roger West Takes Flight (Omnibus) — 60p
- ☐ 18290 3 Accident for Inspector West — 30p
- ☐ 18603 8 Holiday for Inspector West — 30p
- ☐ 15083 1 Murder London–Miami — 25p
- ☐ 17846 9 Murder London–New York — 35p

All these books are available at your local bookshop or newsagent, or can be ordered direct from the publisher. Just tick the titles you want and fill in the form below.

CORONET BOOKS, P.O. Box 11, Falmouth, Cornwall.
Please send cheque or postal order, and allow the following for postage and packing:

U.K. and EIRE—15p for the first book plus 5p per copy for each additional book ordered to a maximum charge of 50p.

OVERSEAS CUSTOMERS AND B.F.P.O.—please allow 20p for the first book and 10p per copy for each additional book.

Name ....

Address ....

....